BOOK 4

I0584315

JENNA AND THE EYES OF FIRE

THE ITURIA CHRONICLES

J.B. MOONSTAR

BOOK 4

JENNA AND THE
EYES OF FIRE

THE ITURIA CHRONICLES

J.B. MOONSTAR

The Little
Horsemen™

Published By: The Little Horsemen an imprint of 4 Horsemen Publications, Inc.

The Little Horsemen Publications
℅ 4 Horsemen Publications, Inc.
PO Box 419
Sylva, NC 28779
4horsemenpublications.com
info@4horsemenpublications.com

Cover & Illustration by Jenn Kotick. Contact for commssions at Jkotickart@gmail.com .

Typesetting by Michelle Cline

Library of Congress Control Number: 2021941355

Paperback ISBN-13: 978-1-64450-248-8
Hardcover ISBN-13: 978-1-64450-650-9
Audiobook ISBN-13: 978-1-64450-247-1
Ebook ISBN-13: 978-1-64450-249-5

DEDICATION

To Dad, thank you for all your love and support.
You are my hero.

Dear Reader,

It has been a few months since Jenna's first adventure into Middle Forest, and Jenna's grandfather has come to live with her family. When the hunters return, searching for magical creatures, Jenna must protect her new forest friends.

Jenna learns her grandfather has been here before, and his knowledge of the past can help with her mission. However, it also puts him in danger.

How can she protect him and her friends without revealing her secret identity? And what if saving her grandfather means Jenna must stop the hunter from ever leaving the forest again?

Sincerely,

Knocker,

First Guard to Ituria

TABLE OF CONTENTS

Chapter One

DANGER RETURNS TO MIDDLE FOREST

"When I was young," said Grandpa, starting one of his many story-telling sessions, "we went barefoot, only wore shoes to school, none of those fancy sneakers. I remember going into the woods with only my knife, a cooking pan, and a pack of matches. I would stay out 'til I had something to take home."

As Grandpa continued, Jenna smiled; she really enjoyed her Grandpa's stories. Since he moved in a few weeks ago, they had made a practice of going out into the back yard after dinner and sitting in the lawn chairs near the forest. He grew up in a world so different than hers and had a unique point of view based on the many challenges he had overcome; some she could not even understand.

"When you go hunting for gators, you have to go out at night. You have to shine your flashlight into the canal and look for the reflection in their eyes. Look at every set of eyes you see, make sure they are small. If you see a big set of eyes, that's the momma, and you don't want to grab one of the babies when she is nearby. Make sure you shine your light on the sides of the canal too, just to make sure momma isn't sitting on the shore."

"So, did you stay out all night, Grandpa?" she asked.

"Many times, I would stay out for days, caught a few gators, trapped a few rabbits, whatever I could get. My dad died young, so it was just my mom and us three kids, my brother and sister and me. We lived with our grandparents, and we helped them when we could. Grandpa would take the gators I caught and sell them to the tourists. Do you remember the movies about monster gators in the New York sewers? Well, that was probably one of my gators they were writing about."

They both chuckled. Jenna was intrigued, wanting to know more. "So how big do you think a gator could get in a New York sewer—as big as they put in the movies?"

"Well," said Grandpa, "I don't know about the fifty-foot-long ones they show on the movie screen, but when I was a kid, no one touched the big gators—too dangerous, so they got really big. Some got over 20 feet long—that was 2 feet of snapping jaws you wanted to avoid at all costs." Grandpa's eyes shined as he talked about his childhood adventures. Then, he leaned back in his chair and closed his eyes, smiling as he remembered his adventures from long ago.

Jenna knew when he closed his eyes, just to let him rest for a little bit. He would wake up again in a few minutes and go right on with the story, like he hadn't fallen asleep. Meanwhile, she looked out into the forest, seeing if she could see any of the animals who lived there.

Remembering back a few months ago, the magic of the forest changing her into a wolf to rescue Ituria from human hunters in the forest. She would have thought it was a dream, except she still had the scar on her shoulder. Somehow, the forest had needed her, and she wondered, *will it ever need me again?*

"Where was I?" said Grandpa, waking back up. "Oh, yeah, hunting and fishing. My mom was always happy when I would bring home meat for the table, except one time, when I brought back this big old snake. It stunk so bad, she said no way, take it out back and bury it! I guess I waited too long to go home that time." Grandpa chuckled again.

"Sounds like you had a lot of fun," said Jenna, smiling again and glad she could share Grandpa's memories. "Don't forget you have a trip coming up, another adventure! Mom and Dad are taking you to the doctor's office for your check-up to make sure your heart is still ticking, and you'll have to stay overnight for this one. You'll need to get inside soon and pack a bag."

"You're right," he said. "But I think I'll sit out here a few more minutes."

With that, Grandpa settled in for another short nap. Looking out into the forest, something caught Jenna's eye. There was some movement along the edge, something small, but it was looking back at them. She could see the eyes. What had Grandpa said, light makes the eyes shine. The light from the porch caused the eyes of whatever was out there to glow in the dark. Now there were two sets of eyes, both small, both looking in her direction.

She rose from her chair and took a step toward them.

Instantly, they darted off into the darkness.

She returned to her chair and looked at Grandpa, the shadows hit him in such a way that he looked like a big bear, with the outline showing bear ears and a snout, and large arms and legs, and a bit chubby in the waist. But wait, she was just imagining it, right? Then she remembered that the forest creatures had told her that she had the shadow of a wolf on her when they watched her from the woods.

Jenna smiled at the thought of a big, cuddly, black bear that looked after her sister and her when they were small. Now it was their turn to look after him. Glancing into the forest, then back at Grandpa, the bear shadow had disappeared; maybe it was just her imagination playing games or wishful thinking.

Sitting out in the backyard, listening to the breeze and the crickets, Jenna closed her eyes too; it was so quiet and peaceful. The soft crunching of leaves next to her chair caused her to open them again. She looked down and smiled as she saw a fox walk up and sit down next to her chair. She knew this fox. *It's Ralphie.*

She looked over to the other chair at Grandpa; he was still sleeping.

She looked back at Ralphie, the fox who visited her several times over the past few months. While they couldn't understand each other since she wasn't a wolf anymore, they still enjoyed sitting together, relaxing near the forest where they first met, back when the forest needed her help several months ago. Tonight, he leaned toward her and dropped a small rock.

She picked it up in her hand and looked at it. It was a small flat rock, about the size of a half-dollar coin.

"Jenna," barked Ralphie. "Ituria has asked that I contact you again and ask for your help. He said the forest magic would help you understand me if you held this rock. We need your help with the hunters. They have come back, many, many of them, and we don't know how to get them to leave." Jenna sat up, startled. Ralphie couldn't talk with her for months, but she could understand him now, and he said Ituria needed her help again.

"I can't leave my Grandpa out here," replied Jenna, hoping the forest magic would help Ralphie understand her. "He's leaving in the morning on a trip with Mom and Dad. Come back after first light, and I can go meet with Ituria."

Ralphie nodded and walked quietly back to the edge of the forest. Jenna leaned over to Grandpa and gently touched him on the arm, murmuring, "Hey, Grandpa, are you ready to go in? Go pack a bag really quick and then you can watch the game."

Grandpa opened his eyes, looked around and said, "I guess you're right. I'll put a few things together for the doctor's visit and then we can watch the game." He loved to fall asleep watching baseball. He would sleep through the game, then Jenna's dad would get him up and help him into his bed when it was over. Not that he always remembered who was playing, but Grandpa said he always liked watching a good ballgame. After she got Grandpa set up with the game, Jenna returned to the edge of the forest to talk with Ralphie.

"Ralphie," she whispered. "Are you still here?"

"Yes," he replied, appearing beside her.

"Ralphie," she continued. "What exactly is going on? Why does Ituria need my help?"

"We need to know the how humans think," he said. "The humans have returned, including their leader we scared away last time. They have lots of guns and supplies, and we don't know why they are here. They don't seem to be hunting for the regular animals. They take trips all over Middle Forest, like they are looking for something in particular. It might be Ituria." The worry in his voice was apparent.

Jenna thought back to when she had first seen Ituria. He was locked in a cage and had been shot in the leg. With the help of his animal friends, Jenna was able to free him and return him home. Ituria would make a fine trophy—he was a majestic white unicorn with a golden horn rising out of his forehead. He had gotten away from the hunters once, and now they were back to reclaim their prize.

"It could be," she replied, echoing Ralphie's worry as many questions formed in her mind. "Did they have any big cages, like the one we found Ituria in before?" *Are they trying to catch him alive or are they planning on shooting him?* Then, she continued, "What do they have besides their guns? Did you see anything else?"

6

"I couldn't see anything else I understood. I did not see a big cage thing, as you call it, or the net like the one Ituria was trapped in before." Ralphie stopped to think, then asked very slowly, "Do you think they plan on killing him this time?"

"Ralphie," Jenna said. "Go back to Ituria and tell him I will meet him in the morning. Then come back here at first light and I'll come back with you. I'll see if I can find out anything else tonight about why the hunters are back."

Ralphie nodded and darted off into the forest.

Jenna turned and headed back inside. *It's going to be a long night.*

Chapter Two

SEARCHING FOR CLUES

Jenna couldn't think of sleep. She went into her room and turned on the computer. She started searching for anything that could identify why there were hunters searching through Middle Forest. *Okay, not Middle Forest*, that's what the animals called it. To humans it was called the Frazier Falls Conservation Area. So she started her search there.

"Frazier Falls Conservation Area" – what did that turn up? There were a lot of articles about the area, but nothing seemed to help. Frazier Falls was named after one of the first settlers in the area, Mac Frazier, and the falls and lake area covered the southern portion of the conservation area, which covered approximately 28 square miles overall. Most of the conservation area was made up of woodlands, with a river running through the middle that ended in the waterfalls running into Angela's Lake.

What else was there that might be used by the hunters to track and kill Ituria? Jenna also kept searching for information that might help Ituria hide. One article described numerous caves near the falls. *This might help*, Jenna thought. *But only if the hunters did not realize where they are.*

Then Jenna spotted several news reports from a few months ago. A few hunters had gone into the area and returned telling incredible stories. *What are they saying?* One claimed he saw a unicorn; another was convinced the trees themselves could kill animals. The group was led by an Ike Monnihan. Jenna did a search under "Ike Monnihan". Soon she found what she was looking for:

> **Wanted: Brave men to go on a quest for a dragon. Last seen in the Frazier Falls Conservation Area. Departing on October 22nd. Apply now! All profits will be split equally between adventurers brave enough to apply.**

Jenna gasped and leaned back in her chair, her mind racing. He had seen Knocker! That was the prize Ike was after. They were going to search Middle Forest until they found him. What could Jenna do to protect him?

Jenna leaned forward again and searched for more information on this Ike Monnihan. She had seen him and knew he was an experienced hunter; he wouldn't fall for simple tricks like the others did.

Reading the numerous articles, she learned many years ago he was well known for leading hunts on almost every continent, Africa, Asia, North and South America. He was always looking for the perfect trophy to bring home. He preferred killing the animal, rather than trapping it, easier to kill the animal and take the trophy home. He was getting older though, and it looked like he wasn't as busy anymore; maybe he wasn't having as much success as he had early in his career.

Jenna's dad had warned her that the Conservation Area had recently been opened for a few days a year for "Hunting Season" as they called it, with the organizers claiming it would help keep the population of predators from coming into the new subdivisions being built around it. People were moving into the land north of the Conservation Area and were afraid of the wolves living there, so they supported the hunting season.

This made Jenna angry, just another senseless way to kill innocent animals. After all, the animals had been there first, and it was the humans who were intruding. Jenna realized Ike had snuck in a few months before, so he could get the upper hand on any hunting to take place, and he had seen plenty!

Now it was officially the hunting season, and Ike had two days left of open hunting in Middle Forest, more than enough time to find Knocker unless he was stopped. She turned back to the computer, what else could she find out about him? Was there anything in all these articles she could be used to make him leave?

After an hour of reading about his exploits and the thousands of animals he'd killed for sport, she came across a small story about one of his expeditions into Canada. He and three men entered the forest looking for moose, but only he and one of the men returned. They had to explain to the authorities what had happened as the bodies of the other two men were never found.

Ike claimed a wolf pack attacked their camp at night. He said he and the other survivor climbed into the trees and stayed there for days until the wolves left. The other two must have been eaten. The investigation into the matter could not prove or disprove Ike's story, as there were no signs of struggle in the campsite, no bones, clothing, or any trace of the two men. When questioned, Ike was very evasive about why he didn't shoot the wolves, and his story conflicted from what the other man said happened.

This must be why he was not hired for any expeditions, Jenna thought. His reputation had been ruined when he lost his customers, something that was not acceptable when people go out for an outing expecting to return home with a trophy. Ike was out to prove he was the fierce hunter he had been in his youth. Could this be used against him? Or did it make him even more dangerous?

What did the other guy say happened?

She found the answer in another article. The other survivor, a Michael Pontain, said the four men were sleeping around the campfire, but the fire had gone out; it was very dark. A loud noise woke him up, along with some howling that could have been wolves. It woke Ike up also, and rather than pull his gun at whatever was approaching, Michael remembered Ike running away into the forest, leaving the others behind to fend for themselves.

Michael was a photographer and didn't have a gun on him, so when he saw Ike run, he jumped up, yelled for the others to wake up, ran a few yards away from the camp and climbed a tree as fast as he could. Michael remembered hearing a lot of growling and screams but couldn't see what was happening in the dark; however, he believed the other two were eaten by wolves or possibly a bear. The article continued, saying there was talk that the brave "Ike" was really a coward and ran away rather than protect his party, and this basically shut down his expedition business.

That was several years ago, and now Ike was back, hungry to make a big kill to restore his reputation. It would be extremely hard to stop him. Jenna turned off the computer and tried to get some sleep. It was going to be a long day ahead. She was worried about the dangers she and her friends would face trying to stop Ike from finding and killing Knocker.

Chapter Three

CREATING A COVER STORY

After a few hours of sleep, Jenna woke with a start. *What time is it? Okay, only 5:48 a.m.* She had a little time before everyone woke up at 6:00 a.m., ate breakfast and her parents and Grandpa took off on their trip. Her sister, Sandy, who was four years older, would be staying home with her. Jenna and her sister had grown much closer since the last time Jenna had been transformed into a wolf by the magic of Middle Forest. Hopefully, she would understand why Jenna had to go back and would cover for her with Mom and Dad.

Jenna went into Sandy's room and woke her up quietly. "Sandy," she whispered, gently shaking her sister's shoulder. "I need to talk with you."

Rolling over toward Jenna, Sandy slowly opened her eyes. "What?" she said sleepily, "What time is it? What's going on?"

Jenna sat down on the bed next to her and said in an excited whisper, "My fox friend returned last night, warning of hunters roaming the forest. I learned from the internet one of them is the same hunter as last time, and he's after Knocker. I have to go back and help them!"

"Knocker," she repeated, trying to wake up. "Who's Knocker?"

"Knocker is the dragon I told you about. He lives in the forest and protects the animals."

"Oh, okay," Sandy said. "Now I remember. But what can you do to help him?"

Jenna's voice raced as she explained, "The animals don't know the hunter is after Knocker and will look to Knocker for protection. However, once Knocker appears, the hunters will kill him. Even though he is a dragon, he would be no match for bullets. Ike wants a trophy and will kill Knocker to show off what a great hunter he is. I've got to do something!"

"But what will you tell Mom and Dad?" Sandy questioned. "You can't tell them you're going to go into the forest and help the animals; or that you'll probably turn into a wolf. It's wolf hunting season now. I don't know if you're thinking this one through. There will be hunters out there ready to kill you too!"

"Maybe I don't have to turn into a wolf," Jenna suggested. "Perhaps I can stay human and still help. I don't know, but I have to try. I at least have to let them know why Ike is there and help plan how to prevent him from succeeding on his quest."

"Okay," Sandy said, then asked again. "What will we tell Mom and Dad?"

"If I'm only gone for the day, they will never know I'm gone. They are taking Grandpa to a doctor's visit and will be gone all day today and all morning tomorrow, returning tomorrow afternoon sometime after lunch. Can you cover for me?"

"Girls, time to get up," called their mother from the hallway. "We've got a busy day today and need to eat early and get on the road. Come have some breakfast."

"Okay, Mom," replied Jenna loudly. "We'll be there in a minute." Then she turned back to Sandy and whispered, "Will you cover for me?" Jenna's eyes pleaded for Sandy to say *yes*.

"If you promise not to get yourself shot by some hunter, I'll cover for you. But you must be careful!" Sandy whispered back, her voice full of concern. "Remember, if you are a wolf, then you are a target. Try to stay safe, my human sister, and get home safe before tomorrow at 1:00 p.m. Promise?"

"Promise. Thanks!" said Jenna and gave her sister a heart-felt hug.

Jenna had breakfast with her family. She found it hard to sit there and be calm; she wanted to jump up and run out the back door, where she was sure Ralphie was waiting for her. But she had to stay and eat breakfast and wait until her parents and Grandpa left on their trip before she could do anything.

"So, Jenna and Sandy, what are you going to do while we're gone?" said Mom. "Have any plans?"

Jenna and Sandy briefly glanced at each other. *What's the right response to this question?* They had to keep their stories straight.

"I don't know," said Jenna, trying to remain calm. "I might catch up on my reading. I have several new books from the library I got last week."

"I might make some cookies or something, if that's okay with you," said Sandy.

"Sounds good. Remember you can always call us if anything comes up. We'll be in Bridgeport overnight, but I'll have my cell phone if you need us."

"Thanks, Mom," said Jenna. "We'll be fine. Don't worry."

"Remember, don't go into the forest," warned Dad. "It's hunting season. I don't want either of you getting mistaken for a wolf and getting shot. There's a lot of crazy people out there. Just stay around the house. Okay?"

"We'll be fine, Dad," replied Jenna, trying to sound unconcerned. "You take care of Grandpa."

Sandy looked at Jenna but didn't say anything else.

As soon as they left, Jenna grabbed a backpack and threw a few items in it—some matches, a knife, a flashlight, some granola bars, a bottle of water, whatever she could think she might need for a trek through the woods. She made sure to take the special rock Ralphie had given her, putting it in her pants pocket so it would not get lost.

"Sandy," said Jenna, smiling at Sandy as she headed to the back. "Don't worry about me. Middle Forest needs my help, but it will protect me. I'll be back by 1:00 p.m. tomorrow. I promise. I'm looking forward to some cookies!"

Sandy was still worried. "Please be careful, like Dad said, there are going to be a lot of crazy people out there—with guns! Do you like chocolate chip?"

"I love chocolate chip cookies!" Jenna exclaimed, smiling again.

"Okay, be back here by 1:00 o'clock tomorrow, and I'll have a whole plate of cookies waiting for you and some lunch too!" Sandy was trying to sound happy, but Jenna could hear the worry in her voice.

"That's a deal. See you tomorrow by 1:00 o'clock," Jenna called out as she headed out the back door toward the forest.

Chapter Four

TRIP TO ITURIA

J enna was only in the forest a few seconds when she saw Ralphie running toward her.

"Hi, Ralphie, I'm here!" she called out, waving her hand.

"Hi, Jenna, where have you been?" he replied. "The sun has been up for a while now."

"I had to wait until my parents left the house with my grandpa. I came as soon as I could. Where are the hunters? Has anything changed since last night?"

"Last night," Ralphie replied, "the hunters were near the north edge of Middle Forest, where Trent and Ranco were shot, and you were able to save Trent. They stayed there all night and set up a camp like they did last time. This morning they left their camp and are moving south, possibly toward their old campsite, but I don't know where they'll end up."

"I need to get to Ituria and Knocker as soon as possible. Also, I need to stay in human form because there are going to be a lot of hunters entering Middle Forest today, and they will be looking for wolves," Jenna responded, talking quickly, wanting to catch Ralphie up on what she had learned last night. "I found out the lead hunter is the one who was here last time and saw Knocker. He's after Knocker, and we need to tell him to make sure he stays hidden."

Ralphie stopped in his tracks and stared at Jenna. "They're after Knocker?" he stammered. "Knocker has taken up his position in front of Ituria's entrance and is planning on fighting whoever tries to get to Ituria. We need to hurry!" Ralphie turned and ran back into the forest.

Jenna, still in her human form, raced after him. Jenna followed Ralphie as he headed southwest, toward Ituria's home. It was about two miles from Jenna's house, but she could make it if she paced herself. It would have been easier as a wolf, but she would be more vulnerable to the hunters, who were looking for a wolf to shoot. Hopefully, she would be seen as one of many hunters joining the hunt.

After about twenty minutes, they came to the Frazier River, and she looked around for a good place to cross. It wasn't deep, only about 15 inches in most places. Still, she didn't want to get her shoes wet and looked for a fallen tree she could use as a bridge. Ralphie had the same idea and ran down the bank toward an old tree stretching most of the way across the river.

"Jenna," he barked. "Follow me over the tree and then a short hop to the other side."

Jenna did as Ralphie instructed and was able to get across. It was only a few hundred yards to Ituria's cave now, and she ran as fast as she could, keeping up with Ralphie. She remembered the path in front of Knocker's cave, where Ranco and his pack members had hidden, and remembered how Knocker scared the wolves away from Ituria's home. She had to get there before anything happened to Knocker.

As Jenna got closer to the entrance, she slowed down a little. She looked around quickly to see if she could detect Knocker in the area. He had never seen her as a human before and might not recognize her. Ralphie stopped in front of the path to Ituria's home.

"Come on," he cried. "Let's hurry!" Then he turned into the path.

"Okay," Jenna replied, then took off after him. She knew this was a magical path, and if she didn't keep up with Ralphie, she might get lost. But only a few feet into the path, she felt something grab her around her waist and lift her into the air.

"Knocker!" cried Ralphie as he watched Jenna float in the air. "Is that you? It's okay, it's Jenna!"

Jenna was suspended in the air for a few seconds, while she heard and felt someone breathing in and out deeply near her. Then she was gently put back onto the ground.

"Jenna," she heard Knocker say. "It is good to have you back. I did not recognize you in your human form."

Jenna looked around. She didn't see Knocker. She looked up, down, back, everywhere. Where could he be?

"Jenna," his voice continued. "You seem confused. You can't see me because Celeste put an invisibility spell on me this morning. When

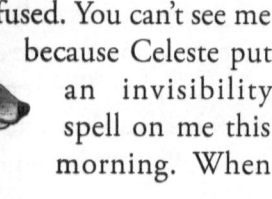

20

Ralphie returned last night with news of the hunters, we knew extra precautions had to be taken. Let's return to Ituria's home so we can talk."

"Okay," said Jenna, staring into the path in front of her. "I'll still follow Ralphie in. I can see him. We do need to talk. I know why the hunters are here, and it's not a good thing."

Since Ralphie knew the path, it was a quick jog up to Ituria's home. Ituria, Celeste, two majestic white unicorns, and Trent, a large grey wolf, were waiting out front for them.

"Welcome back, Jenna," greeted Ituria. "You do look different today than when we last saw you. Thank you for coming back to talk with us. We're hoping you can help us with this new problem—the band of hunters have been prowling Middle Forest since yesterday morning."

"Greetings, Ituria, Celeste and Trent," Jenna replied. "I am glad to come back to help and also glad at this point to be in human form and that you can hopefully understand me."

"Yes, Jenna, we can understand you," replied Celeste. "When Ralphie came by last night, he gave you a translation stone to allow you to be able to communicate with us, even in your human form. As long as you have it with you, we can talk as we did before."

"So many magical things I don't know about Middle Forest. I'm really impressed Knocker can be made invisible. That's a good thing, too. You need to know that for another two days, there will be hunters roaming all round Middle Forest looking for wolves

21

or anything else they can kill. I also found out the main hunter here is the same guy we chased off last time, an Ike Monnihan, and he remembers seeing Knocker and has brought a bunch of hunters here with the promise he will show them a dragon."

"Why are the hunters here looking for wolves anyway?" asked Trent. "What reason would they have to do this. We haven't been hurting them."

Jenna turned to Trent to answer. "I know your pack hasn't done anything," Jenna replied, "but there is a new set of human houses being built in North Forest, and the humans have seen wolves up there, and they are afraid of them. Once humans get afraid, their reasoning goes away, and they panic. Middle Forest, or as the humans call it, Frazier Falls Conservation Area, has always been off-limits to hunting as long as I can remember. However, since Ike left claiming there were wolves in here as well as North Forest, the humans want to get rid of them all. It might be why Ranco was here in the first place. His pack was being chased out by the new humans moving in."

"How long will the hunters be here?" asked Ituria.

"The hunting ban in Middle Forest has been lifted for three days, and there are two days left where hunters will be invading all areas, looking for wolves or anything else they can find. They are only supposed to be hunting for wolves, but most hunters are always looking for something to take home."

"How long can you stay to help?" asked Knocker, still cloaked by the invisibility spell.

"I have to be back by mid-day tomorrow, or my parents will find out I'm out here. My dad told me I'm not to be out here during the hunting season, as I might be shot by one of the hunters." Jenna continued, "I will do the best I can while I'm here, though, to help you develop a plan. My sister knows I'm here, but I promised her I wouldn't get hurt and would be home by mid-day tomorrow. I need to keep my promise."

"We will do our best to protect you and get you back on time," replied Ituria. "Let's get some food and discuss what you know and how we can use it to protect the animals and Knocker."

Nodding, they turned and went into Ituria's cave.

Chapter Five

WHAT LIES AHEAD

E ven though Jenna had been to Ituria's cave before, as she entered today, she was still very impressed. She looked around, seeing the stream running through the left side, piles of food gathered for the animals to eat, and the light shining down from the openings in the sides of the cave. Ituria motioned for them to come over to the right side of the cave. Ituria, Celeste, Trent, Ralphie and Jenna sat down in a circle, leaving a lot of room for Knocker, even though they could not see him.

Jenna started out. "I know why the hunters are here," she said quickly. "Ike remembers seeing Knocker here the last time he was in the forest, and he is back to kill him and take him back as a trophy."

"It was a good thing we made you invisible, Knocker," said Ituria. "Otherwise, you may have been seen and shot. What do you know about the hunters?" he continued, directing the question to Jenna. "You said he was here last time, was he one of those you chased off?"

"Yes," Jenna replied, nodding her head. "He was the leader of the other group; he is the same one who shot Ranco and Trent. He's convinced four others to join him on a quest to find a dragon and regain his reputation." She paused for just a moment, then continued a little slower. "I learned he used to be a famous hunter, but something happened in Canada a few years ago and now no one wants to go out hunting with him anymore. Something about losing two of his group to wolves or bears."

"This is very interesting," Ituria said, pausing to think for a moment. "I heard a story from the elders a few years ago. They wanted to teach a reckless hunter it was wrong to hunt and kill animals for no reason other than to hang them on the wall."

"The two elder bears changed themselves into human form and hired this hunter to hunt with them in what you call Canada. We call the area the Highlands. At the last minute, a fourth person joined the group," he continued, "so they had to put on a special performance to make the other human think they had been eaten by wolves, and it was the elders' actions Ike was running away from when he ran from the camp." Ituria paused to consider the two stories. "This may have been the same hunter. If so, at least we know what type of person he is."

"It sounds like the same man," Jenna agreed. "Why did that frighten him? When we were trying to scare him, he didn't seem to be afraid of anything."

"The elders have special powers," Ituria explained. "They can penetrate your thoughts and dreams, make you hear and see things that are not really there. The elders who visited him were two large grizzly bears who lived in the Highlands. They have been around longer than I can remember, and they are part of the group of elders called the Eternal Protectors."

"But what can we do to get him to leave?" asked Trent. "It looks like he has a new group of hunters with him."

"There are a total of five hunters," said a voice out of nowhere. Knocker's voice continued, "I have been to their camp and there are two younger men and three older men. They don't seem to know each other very well, which may be something we can use to our advantage."

"Last time you were able to scare them away with a few tricks with the help of the local trees," Knocker continued. "However, I don't think it will work so well this time. Ike has been through it before. We will have to come up with something else."

"The elders are too far away to help us," Ituria stated to the open space where Knocker's voice was coming from, "but I remember they were able to scare Ike by placing nightmares in his head while he was sleeping."

"I have heard of this action by the elders also. But I wonder," Knocker's voice paused, then posed the question, "What can we do to make Ike leave and never return? If Ike feared the nightmares in Canada, we may need to use that again. Do you remember what images were put into his head by the elders that would make him react like he did?"

"I think they used images of the animals he had killed, all coming back to life and coming after him," Ituria replied, then turned to look at Celeste.

"Celeste, you also have some psychic powers, but I don't know if you are able to do that."

Celeste shook her head. "No," she replied. "I don't have the power to create nightmares in humans."

"Trying to scare Ike isn't enough," Ituria continued. "We need to force them all to leave and not return. We must go back to their camp and figure out what will work this time." Ituria looked at Jenna. "Are you up to going to the camp so you can overhear their conversations and help us come up with a plan?"

Jenna nodded again. "Yes, but not as a wolf. It would be too dangerous."

"I agree you should not be in the form of a wolf," he continued, "but your human form won't work either. We can give you invisibility for a short period of time, like we did for Knocker, but it will wear off on you quicker because you are not of Middle Forest."

"That would be okay with me," Jenna agreed. "I only need to be invisible for a few hours, until we figure out the best way to get them out of here."

"I can handle that part," Celeste replied.

Celeste stood up and walked over to a shelf. Her eyes focused on a bottle, and it started floating in the air, making its way to Jenna and hovering in front of her. "Jenna," she said. "Drink about one-quarter of this bottle."

Jenna swallowed the medicine; it was sweet and fruity.

"Stay still for a minute while the potion takes effect," Celeste said.

Jenna felt a little tingly and confused for a minute or two. Then she looked down at her hands—or where her hands were supposed to be—and they were gone!

"Okay," said Knocker. "I probably should have picked you up before you went invisible. Stay where you are, and I will come over there and stand next to where you were. You can then reach out and find me and climb on my shoulder. That way I won't step on you, and we can travel to the camp."

"That is probably true," said Jenna, realizing when they were both invisible, they could not see each other. "Tell me when you get next to the spot I was at. I won't move."

Jenna felt something move close to her and reached out. "I am here," she heard Knocker say. She felt Knocker's strong right front leg and climbed up onto his shoulder. Once she was seated, Knocker called out, "We will be back soon!" as they took off toward the hunters' camp.

Chapter Six

HUNTERS' PLANS

J enna was surprised at how fast Knocker could move when he wanted to. She remembered him saying he got his name because he "knocked" into things, but she now realized he could be silent and quick. No one would know he was there unless he wanted to be seen or heard.

Soon they were at the hunters' camp. It was a few miles north of the previous camp a few months ago. It was close to where Ike had shot the two wolves, Ranco and Trent, as they were leaving to return home.

There was a big tent set up. Boxes full of canned food and some bags containing other supplies were stacked outside. It was late morning, and the hunters were still out hunting.

"I remember seeing the hunters following the banks of the river yesterday." Knocker commented. "They seemed to be looking for places where animals might hide. They were close to the waterfall last time I saw them. Is there anything you see here we should take with us or hide before they get back?"

Looking around the camp, Jenna saw a box that looked like it would hold ammo. That would be something to get rid of, for sure.

"I see a box that might contain bullets for their guns. I'm going to get down and check. If it is, I'm going to empty the box in the creek and put the empty box back so they won't know anything has changed."

Jenna climbed down off Knocker's shoulder. "Now…don't move," she said to the invisible space in front of her. "Or I won't be able to find you again."

Sure enough, there were several hundred rounds of shotgun shells. Jenna took them down to the creek, pushed over a large rock and dumped them, putting the rock back on top. Even if the hunters found them, they would be soaked and wouldn't work.

"Last time I took their cooking stuff and it really messed up their dinner and put them in a foul mood," Jenna called out to Knocker. "Let's see what they have this time."

Jenna went over to the boxes of supplies. There were cans of food, but also packs of noodles, salt, pepper, and other seasonings, as well as coffee and powdered milk. As she was picking stuff up, it was so weird and creepy how the packages seemed to float through the air as she turned them over to find out what they were. *Something to remember,* she thought.

Jenna took the coffee, powdered milk, salt, and pepper, and dumped them into the creek, letting them wash away. Then she put the empty packages back into the box.

What else is left? Oh yeah, where are the matches? If there was no fire, there was no way to cook. She dug through the box and found two boxes of matches, as well as a can opener. Again, she took them to the

30

creek and put them under other rocks. The matches wouldn't work, even if they found them.

"Jenna," whispered Knocker. "I hear something. Return to me so we can leave camp."

Jenna quickly returned and climbed onto Knocker's back, and they moved further into the woods. It was about noon now, and the hunters were returning to camp for lunch. Although they couldn't be seen, Knocker was large, so they quietly moved even further back so the hunters didn't accidently walk into them for any reason.

"Hey, Ike," said one hunter as they entered the camp. "What are we here for again? We've been here a day and a half and I still haven't seen anything big enough to shoot. Are you sure you just didn't have a bad dream when you were here?"

"Mitch," replied Ike. "Now wait. The dragon didn't come out until after dark last time. We'll go out again in a few hours and stay out until after dark."

"How about we eat first," said another.

"Sounds good, Josh," said Ike. "We have some canned stew there. Go ahead and start a fire and we can heat it up."

"Hey, Bob and Jeremy," called Josh. "Can you go gather some firewood, and I'll get the pan ready for heating up some food."

"Sure," Bob replied, then he and Jeremy left to gather dead branches for firewood around camp. Knocker took a slight step back to avoid them while keeping close enough for Jenna to still hear their conversation.

After a few minutes, Bob and Jeremy had gathered a pile of wood and Jeremy went over to the box to find the matches. "Hey, Ike," called Jeremy. "Where did you put the matches?"

"They should be in the box there with the cans of stew," Ike replied.

"I don't see them," said Jeremy, "Could they be somewhere else? Where should I look?"

"I put them there myself; they've got to be there," said Ike as he stood and walked toward the pile of supplies.

"I don't see the can opener in here either," noted Josh. "Maybe you put them with the matches in another box or something."

"They should all be with the food supplies," grumbled Ike. "Let me take a look."

Ike waved the two younger men away from the supplies and started moving stuff around in the big box, trying to find the matches and can opener. He couldn't find either. "Okay," he said, sounding a little mad. "If someone is trying to play tricks, it's not funny. I keep some matches in my backpack Let me go get them. Then we can eat. If you can't find the can opener, we'll have to have noodles and bacon for lunch."

"Okay," replied Josh. "I'll get some water from the creek and boil up some noodles." Josh took a large pot from the box and walked down to the creek and filled it up with water. He returned, putting it on the grill he had built over the firewood. Once they had the fire going, he could boil the water and make noodles. He then returned and pulled a frying pan out for the bacon, also placing it on the grill.

"Okay," continued Josh. "Ready for the matches so I can get lunch going."

"Here they are," said Ike, taking something from his backpack and handing it to Josh. "Last time I was here, the little varmints in the woods stole my matches, so I always carry a separate box in my backpack."

"Thanks," replied Josh. "We should have something to eat in about twenty minutes."

"So, what happened last time you were here?" asked Mitch. "I didn't think they allowed hunting here until now. What would you be doing here, other than hunting?"

"I followed a large wolf down from the north and didn't know I had crossed into the conservation area. You know I wouldn't have been here otherwise. I knew there was no hunting here that is until they opened up this three-day season." Ike paused, then stood up. He looked around at the others and continued, "This hunting season is because of me, you know. I am the one who saw the wolves here and actually killed one of them. Made the legal people realize something needs to be done to protect the people moving into the area, and we need to get rid of the dangerous animals."

"Are you sure you weren't trespassing?" argued Mitch. "You have been known to break the rules when you wanted to, as long as you didn't get caught."

"Mitch," Ike replied with anger. "I don't break the rules. I do my best to get my customers what they are looking for, just like you do. They were hunting a wolf, and we accidently ended up in the conservation area; we camped not far from here last time."

As Jenna overheard this conversation, she could tell Mitch and Ike didn't really get along well and was wondering why Ike would bring him along.

"Then tell us again how you came to see a 'dragon' here," asked Mitch sarcastically. "I want to hear it again."

Chapter Seven

TALES OF A DRAGON

"You're always so negative!" said Ike, frowning at Mitch's taunting. "I did see a dragon, or some beast so big it couldn't be anything else. It was right after we broke camp and headed north. There were two wolves squaring off, ready to fight. I shot them both, but when I went to grab them, a large dragon came out of the forest, running at me and my party, and roaring. At that point, to protect my party of course, we left the wolves and headed out as fast as we could. We're camping now on the spot where I saw it."

"So, you high-tailed it out of there, scared of something, and created this dragon story to cover your tracks," scoffed Mitch.

"But what did he see?" asked Bob, looking at Mitch. "If it was something big enough to make Ike turn and run," then looking at Ike, "to protect your party, of course." Turning back to Mitch, Bob continued, "It was at night, so it was dark. Ike could see well enough to see and shoot two wolves, correct?" Bob paused and again looking at Ike. Ike nodded. Then turning back to Mitch, "And rather than claim his prizes, he then left. Something was out there,

35

but what? Mitch, if it wasn't a dragon, what do you think it was?"

"I think it was Ike's imagination," said Mitch, laughing. "Like when he high-tailed it up in Canada, but that time he didn't think about his party. He ran off, leaving them to get eaten by whatever it was he saw in the dark."

"That's enough," growled Ike. "You weren't there in Canada You don't know what happened. I don't even know why I let you come on this trip; I knew you would be trouble from the get-go."

"Ike," said Bob, trying to calm the situation. "I'm not doubting you saw something, but I do have my doubts it was a dragon as I don't think they've ever been proven to even exist. However, I do think you saw something large in the dark, and I'm willing to help you find it. We have tonight and all day tomorrow, so let's all be civil and plan out what we'll be doing tomorrow." Turning to Jeremy by the fire, Bob called, "How's the food coming, son?"

"Noodles are almost done, and bacon's cooking," Jeremy replied. "The salt container was empty, but the bacon is very salty, so I'll mix the two together."

"What do you mean the salt is empty?" shouted Ike. "I only bought it two days ago!" Ike jumped up and quickly walked over to Jeremy by the fire.

"Here," said Jeremy, who seemed a little scared of Ike now, holding out the container, "See for yourself. It's empty."

"That can't be. I know it was full when I packed it." Ike looked a little puzzled. He stood there for a few minutes, thinking.

Jenna was watching, and she remembered last time Ike was in the woods, she had taken his salt, along with his matches, and he might be getting a little worried remembering what had happened last time.

"Food's ready!" called Jeremy. "Here you go." Jeremy handed out four plates of noodles and bacon, one to each of the hunters, and had a fifth plate for himself. The men were quiet as they ate, hungry after a long morning walking through the forest.

Jenna tapped Knocker on the shoulder. "Knocker," she whispered. "Let's go around to the other side of camp. I want to sneak in and move some things around to further confuse Ike. He seems like he's remembering what we did last time, and it may get him worried it is happening again."

Knocker started moving slowly to the other side of camp from where the men ate. When he stopped, Jenna whispered, "Stay here, so I'll know where to find you." Then she silently slipped off his shoulder and quietly walked toward the supply boxes.

Jenna had put all the empty food containers back into the box previously. She looked over at the hunters to see if they were looking her way, but they were too busy eating to look at anything but their food. She picked up the empty coffee containers and stacked them on each other, then added the powdered milk container to the tower, topping it with the empty salt container.

"What is going on!" yelled Ike, and he jumped up and started moving toward the supply boxes.

Jenna ran quickly back to Knocker and climbed on his shoulder. "Go, Knocker!" she whispered urgently, and they took off into the forest.

In the background, she could hear Ike yelling at the others, but couldn't tell what he was saying; then she heard the other men shuffling about. She had gotten Ike's attention. Whether it was a good thing or bad thing, she wasn't sure.

When they were far enough away, Jenna said, "Knocker, let's head on back to Ituria's home. We can discuss more there."

Chapter Eight

PLANS OF THEIR OWN

U pon returning, Jenna and Knocker walked into the cave. Because they were invisible, she announced, "We're back!" Ituria and Celeste looked in the direction of her voice and motioned for them to come over and sit down.

"How about something to eat?" offered Celeste. "It's been a busy day so far and might get even busier." She went over to the food and gathered some fruit and brought it over to the group. "Why don't you and Knocker sit down first?" continued Celeste, "Then we can all join around you, so we don't accidently get in your way?"

"Thank you very much, Celeste," said Knocker as he sat down next to the tray of fruit.

"Thank you, Celeste," joined Jenna. "That sounds really good right now." Jenna slipped off Knocker's shoulder and sat down beside him.

"Okay," Knocker stated. "We're sitting now. Come on and join us."

Celeste, Ituria, Trent and Ralphie sat down in a semi-circle, across from the food and away from where they thought Knocker had rested. There were several leaves filled with food in the middle, and very shortly several pieces of fruit started floating in the air, becoming invisible as Knocker and Jenna enjoyed the meal. Jenna really liked the crispy cracker fruit she remembered from last time and ate several.

"So," said Ituria after a few minutes, to allow them to eat. "What have you learned?"

Jenna responded, filled them in on what she had learned. "We know for sure this was the hunter from the Highlands. Something happened to him in Canada he hasn't shared with anyone. The two older men with him—one doesn't really like Ike; he seems to be there to prove him wrong. The other believes Ike saw something but doesn't really believe it was a dragon He's along to see what Ike might have seen. The two younger people don't seem to know too much about being out in the woods." Jenna paused for a moment. "Do you have anything to add, Knocker, based on what you saw?"

"Well," started Knocker, "I agree with you. It was apparent Ike and one of the older men didn't get along well, based on the tone of their voice to each other. The third older man seemed to be calm, looking for answers, so it may be hard to convince him to leave. The two younger men seemed to be following orders of the older men."

"When you started moving the food containers around above one of the supply boxes," he continued, "Ike looked up and saw them moving, and they appeared to be floating in the air. That's when he jumped up and yelled something. You reacted quickly, and we were able to get away before they came over to the supply boxes."

"Okay," started Trent. "They are looking for something, possibly a dragon. What if they don't find anything? Do you think they will leave? How long are they allowed to hunt in the forest?"

"They have two days left, the rest of today, all day tomorrow and ending at sunrise the day after tomorrow," answered Jenna. "The hunting season was opened for 72 hours and started at sunrise yesterday. Ralphie came by to talk with me last night, and I've been here since this morning. That means two more nights they will be here."

Jenna turned to where Knocker would be sitting. "How long will the invisibility spell last on you? Will it last long enough for you to hide for another two days?"

Celeste responded, "Knocker, you went invisible as soon as Ralphie told us of the hunting parties yesterday morning. The spell only lasts for two days, and I can't put another on you without danger of harm to yourself. You will be invisible until tomorrow morning, but visible before noon. Jenna, I gave you enough invisibility medicine to last for 24 hours, which would mean you would also become visible by tomorrow morning, but I am not sure as we haven't used it on a human before."

Since Jenna and Knocker were still invisible, Celeste was looking at and speaking to the empty space where Jenna's voice came from.

"Okay," Jenna replied. "Then we should be good until tomorrow morning. But I must go home before noon, so we need to decide how to keep Knocker from being seen within the time frame of tomorrow morning until the next sunrise."

"I could go into my cave," said Knocker. "If I stay there, they may not find me."

"But if they do, there is no way out," Jenna said. "I've been there before. Is there anywhere Knocker can hide that has a back exit in case he's found?"

"Ituria," said Trent. "What about the caves hidden by the waterfalls near the lake? Are they big enough for Knocker to hide?"

"That may be a good solution," replied Ituria. "The caves are large, and dark, and there are several entrances and exits. If the hunters discovered the caves themselves, they would most likely get lost and wander around. If they do get close to Knocker, he can leave through another exit."

"I saw the hunters walking along the river earlier today," added Knocker. "Do you think they made it as far as the falls?"

"They did make it to the falls," answered Trent. "They came down the side of the hill and walked the banks of the lake and down the river further past the falls. I was watching them also. They looked at the lake, past the lake and appeared to be looking into the falls and around the sides. They talked to each other for a few minutes and then headed back north, most likely to their camp, where you saw them earlier today."

"They are probably heading to the falls and lake this evening. They too will be thinking—where could a dragon hide?" Jenna said. "Can you see the cave entrance from the lake where they were?"

The conversation continued and several potential solutions were discussed. A plan finally started to take shape.

Chapter Nine

GRANDPA RETURNS

"**S**andy, I'm home!" shouted Jenna as she entered the house the next morning.

"Great, I'm so glad you came home early!" exclaimed Sandy. "Mom called, and they will be here in a few minutes. I wasn't sure what I was going to tell them if you weren't here. I've made the cookies!" she said, smiling at Jenna. "Let's have some now, and then we'll leave the rest for when they get back. They said they were bringing some pizza for lunch."

Sandy looked at Jenna, up and down, then said, "You probably should go change clothes and wash up a bit; it looks like you've been crawling through the bushes." Then, Sandy smiled and gave her a quick hug. "Thanks for coming back safe," she said quietly.

Jenna smiled back at her sister, then looked down at her clothes. *Sandy is right.* While invisible, she couldn't see what a mess she had made of them. There was dirt everywhere, little tears from the branches, and drops of cherry juice from the fruit she was eating earlier this morning. She nodded and returned to her room to grab clean clothes and take a quick shower.

A few minutes after she got out, she and Sandy shared a cookie. Then the rest of the family arrived, and they all gathered in the dining room to enjoy hot pizza.

"Hi, girls! Grandpa passed all his tests with flying colors!" said Mom, smiling at Grandpa. "Doesn't have to go back for another six months. Great job!"

"That's great, Grandpa," added Jenna. "What kind of tests did they do?"

"Jenna," Dad replied quickly. "That's not something you ask."

"No, no, it's fine," said Grandpa. "Gives me something to talk about. They make me walk on the treadmill to make sure my heart can keep up with my legs, or some such nonsense. Then they put me in a big machine and take pictures of my lungs to make sure I can still breathe—although I could have told them I could still breathe," he said, chuckling. "And then, the most difficult test of all," he said, pausing for dramatic effect, "they made me pee in a cup."

Everyone at the table burst out laughing. Grandpa had a great sense of humor, always making a joke about things.

"Well, I'm glad you passed all the tests," said Sandy, smiling. "Sounds a lot easier than the tests I get at school. Anyway, I made fresh cookies for dessert. Who wants some?"

"Sounds good to me," said Mom with a smile. "Thanks for making the cookies. The house smells like fresh baked cookies, a nice, welcome-home smell."

Everyone nodded in agreement and Sandy went to get the plate of cookies.

"Who wants milk with their cookies?" called Jenna as she followed Sandy into the kitchen. "I'm having some."

"Let's have milk and cookies for everyone!" called Mom. "Sounds like a good dessert. We're glad to be home."

After lunch, Jenna and Grandpa went out into the back yard to sit and watch the forest and see if anything was happening there.

"Hey, Grandpa," started Jenna. "Did you ever hunt in the Frazier Conservation area when you were young?"

"Well, yes, I did. When I was younger, in my teens and early 20's—that was a long time ago," he continued. "I did hunt there, before the land around it was developed, no houses for miles and miles. I usually hunted alone, but toward the end of the time I lived in this area, I met a young guy, mid-teens, who wanted to learn how to hunt. He seemed like a good guy, so I showed him how. I showed him my tricks for catching gators and deer, catching fish, how to live out in the woods without getting ants in your sleeping bag; all the stuff you need to know to survive in the woods."

"When I was young, we would hunt for food for the table, nothing wrong with that. I always said, only take what you need, nothing else." Grandpa closed his eyes, like he was thinking about when he was younger, a smile on his face. "Only take what you need," he repeated.

Then Grandpa's face lost its smile. His eyes opened and he looked at the forest. "After I left the area, I heard he turned professional. He went all over the world, using all my tricks to get trophies, and many times he would cut the heads off the animals for a trophy, leaving the rest to rot in the forest. Got me mad. . ." Grandpa again closed his eyes, but there was no happiness in his face; it was a sad look. "Sure wish I could unteach him, would serve him good to have to face animals on their own terms."

"What was his name?" asked Jenna. "Was he from around here?"

"He was from around here, lived a couple of miles away from me to the north," replied Grandpa. "I'm trying to remember his name, heard he had some trouble a few years ago somewhere, don't remember much, but…let's see…Kile, no that's not it, but close…Ike. Yes, Ike…that was his name."

Jenna's mind started racing. Okay, Grandpa knew this Ike that was in the forest now. Did he know anything that would help to get him to leave? What could she tell him and not tell him? How would she even bring up the subject?

"Anyway," he continued, "that was a long time ago. I was glad when they placed a hunting ban on Frazier Falls Conservation. At least some of the animals would be safe. Okay, is it naptime yet? I'm sure there's a ballgame on I could sleep through." Grandpa looked tired after his trip to the doctor's although he would never admit it. He tried to keep a good face on about everything. "No reason to be gruffy," he would always say. "Just do the best with what you got, and don't be wishing for things you ain't got."

"Hey, Grandpa, let's go in and find you a game to watch," said Jenna. "It sounds good to me too."

Grandpa and Jenna went in and found a ballgame on the television, didn't matter who was playing, as Grandpa would be asleep within minutes, and Jenna had too much on her mind to concentrate on what was happening in the game.

"Hey, Dad," called Jenna to the other room. "Grandpa and I are going to watch a game, then take a nap."

"Okay," said Dad. "Not a problem."

Chapter Ten

LEARNING ABOUT IKE

J enna thought she wouldn't fall asleep, but she
hadn't slept at all the night before, so she really
was tired. Once they each got into comfy chairs, they
were both dozing on and off. Jenna's sleep was not
quiet though, her mind constantly turning over the
events of the night before: what she knew now, and
how her own Grandpa had taught Ike how to hunt
in Middle Forest. She would sleep for a few minutes, then startle herself awake. She couldn't keep
her mind from going back to how they had planned
to keep Knocker safe.

After a long discussion, she remembered, it was
decided Knocker would go to Frazier Falls and hide
in the caves. The others would make sure he left no
footprints. While the ground was dry and footprints
were hard to make, Knocker's size made it unavoid-
able he would leave his mark wherever he went.
Once they had decided on the plan, Jenna, Trent and
Ralphie returned to the hunter's camp, making sure
no tracks remained of Knocker sitting out behind
the camp with Jenna.

Jenna woke with a start again. Ike had most likely
been to Angela Lake and knew about the caves; he

had even slept there to get away from bugs and other animals when he was hunting with Grandpa. Perhaps that was what they were talking about when Trent was watching them yesterday. Jenna got her computer out and put it in her lap, maybe there was something else she could find out.

While Jenna was doing another search on Ike, Grandpa woke up. "Hey, Grandpa," started Jenna, "when you were hunting in Frazier Falls Conservation, did you ever go into any caves?"

"There were a couple," Grandpa replied. "Let me think. I remember one cave north of the river fork. It was very dark, and there was no breeze, when meant it didn't go anywhere, so I never went in that one."

Jenna realized Grandpa was describing Knocker's cave, where she first met him. It was probably a good thing he never went into the cave.

"There was another, a large cave, near the lake. You really can't find it if you didn't know it was there. I got lost in there once, took a day to two to find my way out. But there were several entrances, so I followed the fresh air breeze and could find my way out."

"Not much to hunt for in a cave, so I mostly stayed out of them," he continued. "Only mold and mushrooms and stuff that never sees the light of day. There was nothing I would want to bring home."

"Did you ever take Ike to the caves?" asked Jenna, afraid of the answer she might get.

"Well, come to think of it, yes I did," Grandpa replied. "He wasn't all that impressed. We walked by the first; but did go into the one near the lake. Like

I said, it was dark and damp and nothing there to hunt, so we didn't stay long."

"Do you ever keep in touch with Ike?" Jenna asked.

"Nope," replied Grandpa. "Once he started hunting for sport, we had a bad conversation, and haven't talked since. Not much I wanted to say to him after he turned like that. Nothing he could say to me would make it right to kill for no good reason other than to hang something on the wall."

Grandpa closed his eyes again, and this time Jenna did too. She slept until late afternoon, making up for her sleepless night. She woke up in time to help Mom with dinner. After dinner, Jenna and Grandpa went out in the back yard. It was quiet and the sun had gone down, but there was enough light to look through the trees, twilight shining through the branches. Grandpa had closed his eyes, resting again, after discussing how good home cooking was.

Jenna was looking into the woods when she saw something moving quickly toward her.

"Jenna," Ralphie called out. "We need you. The hunters have trapped Knocker in the caves behind the waterfall, lit a fire at one exit and are waiting at the other. There's no opening where he can escape. Please hurry!"

She looked over at Grandpa, but he hadn't moved or opened his eyes.

"Ralphie," she said, rubbing the translation stone in her pocket to make sure it was still there. "What can I do?"

"Come talk to them, make them want to leave, do something!" he pleaded. "We don't know what to do. They broke into two groups, and they lit a fire inside and are standing outside the exits. Knocker is no longer invisible so he can't move without being seen. Smoke is filling the caves, and it may kill him!"

"My grandpa knows this guy from a long time ago. Grandpa taught him how to hunt; maybe he'll have an idea on how to get them to move," Jenna replied. "But you'll need to hide while I ask."

"Okay," said Ralphie, slipping behind her chair.

"Now what is it you need to ask me?" Grandpa asked quietly.

Chapter Eleven

GRANDPA FINDS OUT

J enna jumped. He was awake! What had he heard?

"Well," started Jenna, "I was wondering if you might have some ideas on how to get Ike to stop hunting. He's in the woods now for the hunting season, and I was wondering if you knew anything that would scare him away."

"You and your little foxy friend there, the one behind the chair," said Grandpa, "how are you talking to each other? How can I understand what he's saying?"

"You heard him?" Jenna whispered. "You understood?"

"Yes," replied Grandpa, "and it appears you need to help him with a problem. What is the problem?"

Jenna started talking fast, trying to fit it all in. "Knocker is a dragon…a friend of mine and the fox… he was in the forest…Ike was hunting him…Ike is at the entrance to the caves where Knocker was hiding… Ike lit a fire to smoke him out…Ike is going to kill Knocker…I need to help Knocker!" Her words were running together, she was not sure if what she was saying made any sense.

"Okay," said Grandpa. "Slow down. I won't be able to understand if you keep rambling. And you, hiding behind the chair, you come out too."

Ralphie came out from behind the chair and walked over to Jenna and looked at Grandpa. "How can he understand what I'm saying? Did you give him the stone?"

"No, I didn't," replied Jenna. "I have it here in my pocket." Jenna took it out briefly and showed it to Ralphie, then put it back.

"Back to the problem, okay," said Grandpa, drawing their eyes back to him. "What do you need Jenna for?" Grandpa looked alert, his eyes were bright and he was sitting upright in the chair. "I need to know."

Ralphie looked him in the eyes and started his fox talk. Jenna understood, but would Grandpa? "Jenna has helped us before when trying to deal with humans. She understands how they think. There is only one set of hunters left in the forest, but they have found where we have hidden our friend, Knocker, and I have been sent to seek Jenna's help once again."

"Who sent you?" Grandpa asked, staring right back at Ralphie.

"The Ruler of Middle Forest, Ituria."

"Okay, wait here for a minute, then she can go with you." Grandpa turned back to Jenna. "So now I understand all the questions this afternoon. How did you know Ike was hunting a dragon in the Frazier Falls Conservation area?"

"It was on the internet." Jenna replied. "He put out an ad for anyone brave enough to hunt for a dragon, to join him to hunt here. I saw it two days ago. He was able to get four other people to go with him. They are camping in the forest, and Ralphie says they've found where Knocker's hiding. We tried to hide Knocker this morning in a hidden cave under the falls, in hopes the hunters did not know about it. However, in talking with you, Ike does know about it."

"What do you mean 'we' tried to hide," asked Grandpa with great concern. "What were you doing in the woods during the hunting season? Didn't your dad say to stay out of there?"

"Well, yes," stammered Jenna. "But I had to go. I didn't see any other hunters but Ike and his group, and they couldn't see me."

"Why couldn't they see you?" Grandpa asked, looking straight into her eyes, waiting for her response.

Okay, Jenna thought. *This is getting way too complicated.* Should she just tell him everything? Bits and pieces were slipping out. She was trying to figure out what he should know.

"How can you understand the fox," Jenna asked. "How do you know who Ituria is?" She had to get some common ground to work from. Right now, nothing made sense.

"I know," said Ralphie. "I can see it now. You've met Ituria before, haven't you?"

"Yes," replied Grandpa softly. "I have."

Now it was Jenna's turn to be silent. She looked at Grandpa. She could only see his outline from the porch light, and his outline was not she normally saw. His outline in the porchlight looked like a large bear, just like before. "Grandpa . . ." started Jenna, then she stopped, not knowing what to say.

"Jenna," said Grandpa. "I too have talked with Ituria and Knocker. I stopped hunting in Middle Forest once Ituria became the ruler and made it a non-hunting area. I will help you do whatever you can to protect Knocker and the others."

"However,' Grandpa continued, "I am too old to be running around trying to help, and you will have to be the one to do it. I can see from your shadow you must have met Ituria, because you have the shadow of a wolf around you now."

"We can talk about your other adventures later, but now," said Grandpa, looking at Ralphie, then back to Jenna, "you must find a way to help. Maybe we can come up with some ideas together. But we will have to be quick. Ike will have worked out a plan if he thinks Knocker is in the cave. We will have to outthink him."

"Does your sister know?" asked Grandpa.

"Yes," replied Jenna, "but not Mom or Dad. Sandy saw me change into a wolf a few months ago and covered for me until I returned the next day."

"Well," said Grandpa, "maybe she can cover for us both."

"I don't know," replied Jenna. "Having to cover for me is incredibly stressful for her. I'm not sure what she would do if she knew you were going to wander through the woods."

"Oh, no." Grandpa chuckled. "I'm not going wandering through the woods. But I would like to stay out here, so your friends can keep me advised of what is going on. I will only go into the woods if required. Remember, I'm an old man, and would be an old bear. Old bears don't run too fast." Grandpa smiled, and Jenna finally realized he could help her and the others.

Chapter Twelve

A SECRET ENTRANCE

"Jenna," said Ralphie. "Ituria said you should stay in human form, but I'm not sure if you can run fast enough with only two legs."

"Let's figure out what we can do to help," advised Grandpa. "Then we can decide how she will get there. How many people are in Ike's party?"

"There is Ike and four others," answered Jenna. "Two older men, about Ike's age. Then two young men, they look like they are in their late teens or early twenties. One of the younger hunters appears to be the son of one of the older guys. If the group split, then the father and son probably teamed up."

"When we are at the camp yesterday," Jenna continued, "I emptied all the boxes of ammo into the river. I'm not sure if they know or not yet. They will only have what they have in their guns and possibly pockets. But we don't know what they had with them."

"One of the people in the party—Mitch, seems to be a rival of Ike; they don't get along. Not sure why he brought Mitch along, who seems to be trying to make Ike look a fool for suggesting there is a dragon in the forest. What can we do?" asked Jenna, looking at Grandpa.

"Okay," said Grandpa. "Ike's only weakness is his own arrogance. He doesn't think anything can beat him. We will have to play on that. If he has blocked the exits to the cave, we have to get him to move. Maybe we can separate his party even further, getting him away from the others."

"I agree with Ituria you should remain a human," he continued, "but we are running out of time. Ike may try to go into the caves." Turning to Ralphie, he said, "What were the two groups doing when you left?"

"They had lit fires in front of one of the two entrances to the cave. They didn't seem to want to go in, and were behind some rocks at the second entrance, waiting for something to come out," Ralphie replied.

"He's probably trying to smoke Knocker out. Luckily, the caves are deep, and it will take a long time for the smoke to get to the back. The waterfall is about three miles southeast of here," said Grandpa. "It will take at least half an hour to walk there. Jenna, it is going to be dark, do you think you can find it?" Turning to Ralphie, he continued, "Ralphie, would you be able to get Jenna there?"

Ralphie nodded his head.

Turning back to Jenna, Grandpa continued, "Jenna, listen, there is a third cave entrance on the far east side of the waterfall. There is also an underground river connecting the lake to Ituria's home. Knocker may know but Ike does not; I never showed them to Ike because of his lack of interest since there was nothing to hunt for there. You must enter the cave and make sure Knocker takes the underground river to escape."

"Ralphie, once you get Jenna to the east entrance, hide in the bushes and wait for her to return. Once she contacts Knocker, lead her back home in the dark. I will wait here for your return."

"I will need a flashlight," noted Jenna. "I will tell Sandy that you and I will be out here for a while so not to worry about us."

"Tell her…I'm enjoying the night air," added Grandpa, "and that we will be in later."

Jenna quietly walked through the house back door and found a flashlight on a hall closet shelf. Sandy was just finishing up with the dishes in the kitchen, when she looked up and saw Jenna with a flashlight in hand, heading toward the back door again to leave.

"Hey," Sandy said, walking over to her. "What are you doing?"

Jenna looked at her sister and said, "Grandpa and I will be outside for a while, enjoying the fresh night air. Grandpa says it reminds him when he used to go camping as a kid. If he falls asleep, I will stay out there with him and keep watch."

There was a question in Sandy's eyes and Jenna could see she wasn't quite buying the story. What more could she say, and what should she not say?

As Jenna turned and headed out the back door, she continued, "Tell Mom and Dad Grandpa is okay outside because he is with me and they don't need to worry about him or check on him."

"Jenna. . ." started Sandy, then she paused as she followed Jenna onto the porch outside. "What is going on? Is there something you are not telling me?" The doubt and concern filled her voice.

"Sandy, please listen," whispered Jenna. "I need to go back into the forest. Grandpa said he would wait for me outside until I return. Keep Mom and Dad inside for an hour or two. Tell them Grandpa and I are talking…"

"Wait," interrupted Sandy, anxiously whispering. "What do you mean Grandpa said it was okay for you to go into the woods at night, are you crazy! Why would he say that? What did you tell him?"

"Sandy, I don't have time now; I will tell you later. Please tell Mom and Dad Grandpa and I are outside talking and napping, and you will check on us. They don't need to worry. I know you can do it, just for a few hours until I get back. Please!"

Sandy looked at Jenna, she could tell Jenna was going whether she agreed or not. "But what about Grandpa, is he going to be okay?"

"Yes," Jenna replied. "He will be fine. Nothing to worry about. He will wait outside for me. I've got to go!"

Jenna opened the porch door and ran out toward Grandpa and Ralphie. "Sandy is not convinced, but hopefully she can keep Mom and Dad away for a few hours. I will be back as soon as I can. Thanks, Grandpa," said Jenna and gave him a quick hug and kiss.

Then Jenna and Ralphie took off into the forest.

Chapter Thirteen

RESCUING KNOCKER

Jenna and Ralphie traveled southeast in the dark; luckily there was enough moonlight to help follow the paths. Jenna didn't want to use the flashlight because others would see them. They reached the east cave without being noticed by Ike and his group. Jenna could hear them in the distance as they got close and saw the fire, but she wasn't close enough to understand their conversation. The hidden cave they were searching for had an entrance on top of the falls, rather than underneath, and Grandpa had said Ike didn't know about this entrance.

Jenna leaned down and whispered to Ralphie as she entered the cave, "Okay, wait for me here and I'll bring Knocker back and we can all go to Ituria's cave together using the underground river."

"Okay, Jenna," agreed Ralphie. "I'll wait near the entrance in the bushes for you to get back with Knocker. Be safe!"

Once inside the cave, Jenna turned on the flashlight. She could see a narrow walkway on the east side of the underground river and followed it down toward the falls. Knocker was under the falls, in a cave hopefully not known by Ike. Rather than waterfalls inside the cave, there was a gentle sloping of the underground river, like lots of small rapids.

Sticking to the east side, she slowly descended into the wet musty caverns. There was a whiff of smoke, which got stronger as she went deeper under the falls. She could hear the crashing of the waterfalls in the distance, so she must be getting close to where the two caves met. So far, the path was wide enough for Knocker, so he wouldn't have to try and climb the numerous sets of rapids.

"Knocker," she called quietly. "Are you still here? I've got another way out for you It links to Ituria's home. Can you hear me?"

No answer. She continued down the slippery path, bracing herself on the walls to keep from sliding down the sloped path. She repeated her calls to Knocker and finally got a reply.

"Jenna, what are you doing here?" asked Knocker as he appeared out of a small cave in front of her.

"I know a back way out of these caves that leads to Ituria's home," Jenna replied. "The hunters are trying to smoke you out so you will come out the front entrance, but we can escape out the back. It is big enough for you, but a bit slippery."

"It is getting a little smoky in here," agreed Knocker. "I haven't heard or smelled anything come into the caves. What did you say was happening outside?"

"The hunters lit fires at one of the two entrances and are waiting for the smoke to drive you out the other," Jenna explained quickly. "They must have figured out this is the only place you could hide. They will be there all night if need be. We need to get you out of here."

"How did you find me without the hunters seeing you?" asked Knocker.

"No time to explain," said Jenna in a rushed voice. "Let's get out of here before the smoke gets too bad. We can talk later."

"Okay," agreed Knocker. "You go first, and I can follow you and the light you carry."

Jenna headed back to the high cave where she had entered. It was slow going because they were going uphill on slippery rocks, and some points were so narrow Knocker had to get into the river rapids to get past. It took about fifteen minutes to get out, twice as long as it took Jenna to find Knocker, but at last the moonlight could be seen through the cave entrance.

"Ralphie," whispered Jenna. "We're back. I found Knocker and we are ready to take the river the rest of the way back to Ituria's home. You can come out now and join us." There was no answer.

"Ralphie, are you there?" she whispered again, now worried about Ralphie.

Knocker drew in a deep breath, once, then again. "Jenna," he said in a low voice. "Ralphie is not here. He was here once, but no longer. I also smell human scent around the front of the cave. Something is not right."

Jenna raced through the entrance to the cave, shining the flashlight into the bushes where she had left Ralphie. The ground was trampled, and the leaves and branches were broken and bent.

"Ralphie!" shouted Jenna. "Come back!" She didn't care if the hunters heard her, she had to locate Ralphie.

In response, she heard the high-pitched bark she knew was Ralphie. "Jenna," he said, "my foot became caught in a metal box. The hunters have pulled me over by their fire. Please help!"

Jenna knew she was going to have to confront them to get Ralphie back, and that is exactly what she was going to do.

Turning to Knocker, she said, "You must return to Ituria. You won't be able to help me get Ralphie. I will try and talk them into letting him go."

"I agree I can't help at this point," replied Knocker, "but I will go back and let Ituria know, then see if there is anything we can do to help you and Ralphie." Knocker got into the underground river. "I will get you help!" he said as he disappeared into the darkness, heading north toward Ituria's home.

"Thanks!" called Jenna as she headed out of the cave and headed straight for the hunters' fire.

Chapter Fourteen

CONFRONTING THE HUNTERS

"**H**i!" she called out as she approached. "I'm looking for my pet fox, he got out and I need to find him before he gets hurt." As she was talking, she was desperately searching for Ralphie around the fire and behind the men standing in front of it.

"Hey, little girl," said one man. "You shouldn't be out here at night. This is hunting season, and you could get shot."

"I know," replied Jenna, the fear she heard in her voice was real, "but my pet fox got loose, and I'm afraid someone will kill him before I can find him. Have any of you seen a fox around here?"

"There's nothing here of yours," said a voice Jenna knew belonged to Ike. "So go look someplace else."

"But what about . . ." started a younger man, but he stopped abruptly as Ike's angry glance caught his attention.

"There's nothing here," Ike repeated. "Go home."

Behind a small pile of backpacks came a weak whine, like an animal in pain.

Jenna ran past the hunters before they could react and found Ralphie chained to a tree, the chain attached to a trap which was cutting into his back leg. Softly, she said to him, "Don't talk, Ralphie. I have the stone, and they might understand you." Then, much louder, she said, "Ralphie! I've found you! You're hurt! Oh, no!"

She turned back to Ike and said, "Please, this is my pet, I've had him for years, raised him from a baby, please let me take him home!" Jenna was pleading now, knowing that physically, she could not take on five men. But she hoped she could appeal to some of them, encouraging them to let Ralphie go.

"How do we know he is yours?" questioned Ike. "You could be hunting like the rest of us and want to take our rightfully caught animals."

"Ike," said Mitch. "You are losing it. Give the little kid her pet back."

"How do we know it's hers?" Ike retorted. "Maybe she saw me catch it and now she wants it for herself."

In response, Jenna walked over to Ralphie, looked at him and said, "If he wasn't my pet, would he let me pick him up?" Jenna knew Ralphie could understand her, so she could tell him what she needed him to do. Reaching down, she carefully picked up Ralphie, making sure the trap didn't tear his leg any further.

"If he wasn't my pet, would he let me pet him on the head?" Jenna asked, then started petting Ralphie on the head.

"Ike," said Bob. "It is obvious it is hers. Let her have it. We're not here to hunt foxes anyway."

"Yeah," said Mitch sarcastically. "We are here to hunt dragons, right!" and started laughing. Then he looked at the others and said, "I think we have had enough. Trying to trap a dragon from a cave we don't even know exists isn't working either, is it Ike?"

Now that Jenna had Ralphie in her arms, she was going to see if she could get them fighting with each other so she could slip away.

"Did you say you were hunting for a dragon?" she asked, perplexed. "Where in the world did you get such an idea?"

Mitch laughed again and said, "Yeah, this guy says there are dragons living here—but we haven't seen anything yet."

"Well," replied Jenna. "I've been in these woods many times, and I've never seen anything close to a dragon, except maybe a gator."

"We are not here for gators," shouted Ike. "It was not a gator!" Ike glared at Mitch. "I know what I saw and I'm going to catch it, just you wait and see."

"How do you catch a dragon?" asked Jenna in a small voice as she slowly backed up.

"Yeah, Ike, how do you catch a dragon?" Mitch was enjoying teasing Ike, and continued, "We're still waiting to see!"

"Oh, don't you worry," Ike replied. "When he appears, I'll shoot him and take his head home so everyone knows I was telling the truth! And you, you wait right there!" Ike glared at Jenna. "I caught that fox fair and square and it is mine!"

"How much would you get for him? I will pay you . . ." started Jenna.

Bob put out his hand at Jenna's offer. "No, Ike," he said. "This is her pet, and you are not going to make her pay you to keep it. She's already going to have to pay to get the doctor to fix its leg," Bob walked over to stand between Ike and Jenna, staring at Ike. "You didn't come here for this little fox, and neither did we." Bob looked at the others, then back at Ike. "We came here based on your claims of a wild 'dragon' in this area. Right?" Bob used his fingers to draw quotation marks in the air when he said dragon.

"We've been here almost three days, and I haven't seen anything near a dragon, no footprints, no nothing. Not even the wolves you'd promised roamed all over this place."

"I think we have seen enough," Bob said. "Let's put out the fire and head back to our camp. We can get a good night's sleep before heading home in the morning. Who is with me?" He looked at the others.

Josh and Jeremy both agreed, saying in unison, "I am!"

Mitch wanted to rub it in a little more. "So, you came for a dragon and are now fighting a little girl for her pet. What a great hunter you are!" Then to the others, "Yep, I'm ready to go too. Bob and Jeremy, let's put out the fire and head back to camp."

Jenna started walking away, not wanting to give Ike a chance to press his argument to keep Ralphie. Although she had a flashlight, it was still very dark, and she did not know her way home. She had followed Ralphie to get this far into the woods.

"Okay, Ralphie," she murmured as they got away from the hunters. "Let's go home. I will carry you."

She knew the hunters could still see her if they looked her way, so she started out to what she hoped was northeast and her house. Once they got far enough away, she could check with Ralphie about which way to go.

The hunters were busy putting out the fire and didn't seem to notice as she slipped away. She looked back and didn't see anyone following her and hoped she could make it home. She knew it would take about half an hour to get there.

Once out of earshot, she whispered, "Okay, Ralphie, which way from here?"

"Take the path to the right after the large oak," he replied. "It leads back to your house."

"Thanks," said Jenna. "I'm glad you can help me find my way home. Let's see if we can that trap off your leg."

They worked with it for a few minutes, and Jenna was able to spring the trap open and free Ralphie's leg.

"Thanks! That feels so much better!" Ralphie looked at Jenna and continued, "Thanks also for coming back to rescue me; I was so scared when I felt the metal box close on my foot. I called to you, but you must have been too far away. Did Knocker make it out?"

"Of course, I would come to help you. I am so glad we could get away from them. Knocker did make it out, and he's on his way back to Ituria's cave now."

From behind them, came a threatening voice. "So who is this Knocker?" It was Ike, who came closer and continued, "What are you two hiding from me?" He was about ten feet away now, glaring down at them.

Jenna grabbed Ralphie and started running down the path. Because she was carrying Ralphie, she was slower, and Ike caught up with them quickly, trapping them in a little ravine on the side of the path.

"Now," demanded Ike. "Answer me! What are you hiding? And why can you and the fox talk to each other?"

Chapter Fifteen

CORNERED

J enna tried to remain calm and responded, "Don't be silly. I'm just pretending he's talking to me; I'm doing both sides of the conversation. I'm playing with him."

"No" growled Ike, "I can see you and he are talking, and I can understand him too."

"Do you realize how silly that sounds?" Jenna replied, hoping to sound convincing, not sure if she was succeeding.

"It don't matter," Ike retorted. "I caught him fair and square and he is mine, so hand him over—now!"

"No!" yelled Jenna. "You hunt for fun, you enjoy killing animals with your guns to try and prove to yourself you are brave. You should only take what you need and nothing else. There is no way you need this little fox, and I'm not giving him to you!"

"I only need his skin." Ike smirked. "It's worth a lot to me. Don't worry, I'll kill him quick." The smirk on Ike's face curved into an evil grin, as if looking forward to killing Ralphie.

"I don't have my gun, but I do have this knife!" and Ike quickly pulled out a knife from his holder on his back. It was a hunting knife with a large sharp blade. "So, what are you going to do about it? I told you before, little girls should not be in the woods. Now run home to your mommy!" Ike took a step toward Jenna and Ralphie, he was only a few feet away now.

"I won't let you kill him!" Jenna's voice was full of resolve, but Ike didn't seem to care. Jenna put Ralphie down and stood between him and Ike.

"Little girl," sneered Ike. "I will kill you both. No one will be the wiser. I'll tell you one more time—I caught him fair and square and he is mine—now move!" Ike waved the knife in the air, making several slashing motions, coming close to Jenna's face.

Jenna could feel her anger at Ike growing inside her. There was no way she would let Ike get to Ralphie. She felt another sensation also, it felt like when she was transformed into a wolf last time. She realized the magic of Middle Forest was going to transform her so she could defend herself and Ralphie. In a surprising calm voice, she said to Ike, "this is your last chance—go now or you will regret it."

"Why should I be afraid of you, little girl?" Ike was laughing at her now. "What are you going to do, kick me with your little foot?" He held up his hand with the knife a little higher in the air in case she tried.

Jenna had been standing between Ike and Ralphie, shielding Ralphie. She stared at Ike, and as she transformed into a wolf she leaped and grabbed the hand with the knife in it in her mouth, and bit down hard until he let it go. Then she pinned him down to the ground. He was face down in the dirt, and she was standing on top of his back.

"What is going on?" Ike's eyes were wide open as he tried to turn his head to look at her. "What are you?"

Jenna noticed during her transformation the translation stone had somehow landed on the ground near Ike.

"You are a bad man, hunting and killing animals, wasting their lives just so you can prove to yourself you are a 'great hunter', and you enjoy killing." Jenna wanted to let Ike know what she thought of him, unable to contain her anger any longer. "You don't dare meet the animals on their terms, or you would have been dead a long time ago."

"Let me go, let me go or I will tell everyone you are really a wolf! They will kill you!" Ike was still trying to find a way to get the upper hand in the conversation, but Jenna wasn't buying it. He started to struggle and attempted to move or get away from her, but she moved closer to his face, growling as she stared into his eyes, and he stopped struggling.

"So you think they will believe you? You who claim to have seen a dragon—I don't even know where that came from. And now you're going to tell them the little girl you tried to kill is a wolf? How are you going to explain you tried to kill me?" Jenna tried to figure out a way to let Ike leave where he would not come back into Middle Forest again.

"Listen well, you can swear to me now you will never hunt my friends again, or I can kill you. Like you said before, no one will be the wiser." Jenna waited for Ike's reply.

"Okay, okay," he stammered. "I promise, let me go. I'll leave now, please—let me go!" Ike was scared now. He probably had never faced an animal without his gun and really was a coward. Jenna could tell he was only brave when the odds were stacked greatly in his favor.

"Remember," she replied, "we can see you even if you can't see us. If you come back to this area, I will not let you hurt my friends again—ever."

Jenna knew she could not trust Ike, that he would say anything to get loose. "Should I trust you—no! If you come back, you will regret it. You have been warned. Do not return to this forest." While Jenna said it calmly, she could tell Ike did not take her threat lightly. His head was laying sideways in the dirt, her mouth and sharp wolf teeth only a few inches from his face; he looked like he was going to cry.

Jenna called out, "Ralphie, if you can walk, go ahead and go where we were going before. I will follow you in a moment." Where Ike couldn't see, Jenna used her nose to point to the translation stone, and Ralphie understood he should take it with him. After Ralphie disappeared into the darkness, Jenna turned her attention back to Ike.

"You may go, join the other hunters and leave this area tonight. This is your final warning; we will be watching you. Do not return!" She knew as she let him up with the stone gone he could not really understand what she was saying anymore, but her growls had said enough—no translation stone was needed.

Ike jumped up and took off, running as fast as he could toward the other hunters.

Jenna followed a short way, making sure he did not turn back, then went after Ralphie, picking up the flashlight in her mouth. Her wolf sense could track Ralphie in the dark, and her wolf speed allowed her to catch up with him quickly.

"Ralphie," Jenna growled. "I have scared Ike, but I do not think he is gone for good. Let's go back to my house until they leave."

"Okay," agreed Ralphie. "Sounds like a good plan."

A few minutes later, they were at Jenna's house.

Chapter Sixteen

GETTING HELP FOR RALPHIE

As Jenna and Ralphie approached her house, they saw Grandpa and Ituria talking in the back yard. Ituria was standing behind some trees so as not to be seen if someone looked out the window from the house. Both turned toward the dark forest as she and Ralphie approached.

"Jenna?" called Grandpa into the darkness. "Is that you?"

"Yes," Jenna growled in response, but she was not sure he would understand.

"Are you okay?" Grandpa continued with concern. "Look, I have my own translation stone now, so I can understand you," he continued as he held up a small stone in his hand.

"Grandpa, it's me!" Jenna called as they got closer, "please help Ralphie. He was caught in one of Ike's traps. Ike wants to kill him. The only way I could save him was for Middle Forest to transform me into a wolf. He needs someone to bandage his foot."

"Ralphie," replied Grandpa, looking at the fox. "Come here and let me look at your foot."

Ralphie walked slowly over to Grandpa, limping on one foot. While Grandpa looked at Ralphie's foot, Ituria walked over to Jenna.

"Jenna," he said. "You need to change back into a human as soon as possible. It is not safe for you to remain a wolf."

"But I don't know how," she exclaimed. "How do I do it?"

"You must calm yourself. You are still upset over what has happened. Until you separate yourself from your anger, you will not change back."

"You are right," Jenna agreed. "When I got really angry at Ike, I could feel myself changing. But I had no choice. Ike was going to kill Ralphie, me too, if I didn't turn him over. He was going to…skin him… take his fur and leave . . ." Jenna could not continue, she could not bear to think of what Ike had intended for Ralphie.

"Jenna," said Ituria, his calm voice calling her back to the present. "You must separate yourself from this anger. If Ike shows up here or sees you from the forest, you must be a human."

"Okay, okay," she said as she tried to calm herself down. "But it is difficult. He is a bad man."

Ituria could sense her anger rising again. "Remember how you were calm while helping Trent? Think back to that calm place. You knew there was danger, but you acted calmly and you were able to save him."

Ituria's words pulled Jenna back to when Trent was laying on the ground; he had been shot by Ike. She had seen what needed to be done and worked through her fear to save Trent. She had been transformed into a wolf by Middle Forest because it was needed, but when the need was over, she was transformed back. Ralphie needed her now, and she could best help him by being human.

Jenna closed her eyes and thought about Ralphie and what he needed, what she needed to do now to help him. She looked over at Ralphie. He was laying down beside Grandpa. Grandpa was sitting in a chair, leaning over and trying to wrap a napkin around Ralphie's foot.

Her concern for Ralphie filled her and she knew she needed to help him. She closed her eyes and concentrated—Ralphie needed help and she needed to remain calm and return to her human form so she could go inside and get some bandages for him. Jenna's next sensation was laying on the ground as a human girl. The transformation only took a few seconds once she reached the right state of mind.

"Very good, Jenna," said Ituria. "You are learning to control your emotions, so you will soon be able to control them when you are a wolf and when you are a human."

Jenna took a few seconds to readjust to her new form, then turned toward the house. "I'm going to get some first aid supplies from inside so we can clean up Ralphie's leg," she called softly as she ran toward the porch door.

Jenna tried to sneak in the back door, but she ran immediately into Sandy, who was standing there waiting for her.

"Okay," Sandy said quietly. "What is going on now? I can't really see outside, but I can hear voices, and not only you and Grandpa." Jenna could tell she would have to give some explanation to Sandy but didn't have time to tell her everything now.

"Sandy," Jenna answered. "One of my friends, Ralphie the fox, got caught in a hunter's trap and I got him free and brought him home." Jenna figured Sandy didn't need to know more now. "I need to get some first aid stuff from the bathroom and bandage him up." Jenna started walking past her sister, but Sandy stepped back into her way.

"Jenna," Sandy whispered. "Mom and Dad are in the living room watching a movie. I've been in here pretending to read a book while waiting for you. They were okay with you and Grandpa staying outside, but I'm not sure how the fox can be explained."

"If they ask, I can tell them I heard something outside in our yard and found him trapped," Jenna suggested. "Does that work?"

Jenna thought a second, then added, "and…if anyone asks, I've had Ralphie, the fox, for a few years now, and I have raised him from a baby, okay?"

"Jenna . . ." started Sandy.

"No, not now," Jenna whispered. "Tomorrow I can tell you everything. I promise. It's that tonight there's no time."

"Okay," Sandy agreed reluctantly. "But be careful!"

As Jenna walked by the living room, she saw Mom and Dad had fallen asleep in front of the TV, so she tried to be as quiet as possible to avoid having to explain anything to them.

A few minutes later, she was back outside with some wound cleaner, gauze pads, and an ace bandage. "Ralphie," she called in a soft voice. "Here I come. I've got some stuff to help with your foot." Jenna kneeled next to him and started to clean and bandage his foot.

"Here, Jenna," Ralphie said as he returned the stone. "Keep the translation stone with you for now."

"Thanks, Ralphie," she replied. "Does your foot feel any better now?"

"Yes, much better," Ralphie said. "Thank you for saving me!"

Ituria's ears twitched, and he whispered, "I hear voices in the distance. I will disappear for a little while. I will be within hearing range and can help if needed." Then, Ituria disappeared into the darkness.

Grandpa leaned back in his chair and let Jenna continue with Ralphie's foot. "I hear something too," he said in a low voice. "How many people did you see out there? Sounds like a group of people heading this way."

"There were five in all," Jenna whispered. "But only Ike saw me as a wolf."

"Okay," Grandpa replied. "You lead the conversation, and I will back up whatever you say."

"Thanks, Grandpa," said Jenna, so glad he was here for support. She did not look forward to talking to the hunters again and could only imagine what Ike may have told them.

"There's some lights on over there. I bet that's where she is!" shouted a voice Jenna knew was Ike's.

"It's Ike, Grandpa," she whispered. "He's come after us, probably tracked me and Ralphie here. I would have left wolf footprints on the path."

"Okay," he replied quietly. "Let's blame the footprints on the dog from down the street. You know, the big Doberman named Sunny we see sometimes walking on the sidewalk. Remember he got loose last week, and the owners were looking for him in the woods? The footprints would be about the same."

Jenna nodded her head in agreement just as the five men walked into the back yard from the forest, Ike in the lead. Jenna braced herself for the next confrontation, knowing she had to remain calm, or she would turn into a wolf and confirm whatever stories Ike may have told the others.

Chapter Seventeen

IKE'S CLAIMS

"There she is!" Ike shouted. "Just like I told you. Her and her fox."

"Okay, Ike," Mitch said. "So we see a little girl and her pet. What else do we need to know—we saw her earlier too. Same thing now as then."

"She bit me!" Ike cried out. "Look at my hand!" he continued, holding out a hand wrapped in a towel.

"My fox bit you when you tried to take him from me," Jenna replied.

"She bit me, not that little fox, she's really a wolf, I swear!" Ike desperately pleaded for the others to believe him.

Jenna responded, "Did you tell these men you threatened to kill me if I didn't give you my Ralphie?"

Bob got in front of Ike, looking directly at him. "Did you threaten this girl? I thought we had resolved this issue back by the caves. Is that where you ran off to?"

"He pulled out a knife and said he would kill us both if I didn't hand over my fox. Ralphie was trying to protect me when he bit this man on the hand." Jenna knew she had to remain calm and tried not

83

to let her anger get to her, but she needed to let the others know what Ike had done.

"Ike," said Mitch. "This is even low for you. Did you really pull a knife on a kid?"

"Well. . ." started Ike, then he tried to change the point of the conversation, "but she is a wolf, I tell you, she is the one who bit me."

"So you don't deny you pulled a knife on this little girl?" demanded Bob. "And all for what, so you could kill her pet!" Jenna could see Bob was angry now. "I followed you out here; I've been here for almost three days trying to find this dragon you claim you saw. Now you stoop to threatening a girl to kill her pet so you have something to show for your time! I have nothing to show for my time out here except the knowledge I will never believe a word you say again, ever!"

Bob turned to Jenna and said, "Little girl, I am sorry your pet is hurt. I am sorry I supported this man, but I can assure you that you and your little fox are safe. We are leaving now and will break camp first thing in the morning, and Ike will not be coming back to try and take your pet again."

Bob looked directly at Ike. "Isn't that right, Ike."

Everyone turned to Ike, to see what he would respond.

Ike was furious, glaring at Jenna. "I will not stop until I prove she is really a wolf!"

Grandpa rose from his chair and joined the conversation. "I recognize your voice, after all these years, Ike." He walked over and looked Ike in the eyes. "Do you remember me? I'm the one who taught you how to hunt, told you only to take what you needed and never more. Now you are here threatening my granddaughter. What has changed you so much you would do such a thing?"

"You didn't teach me anything," exclaimed Ike, his disdain for Grandpa showing in his voice. "Hunting for food isn't worth the time. I hunt for prizes, and I've gotten a lot. I'm not going to be like you, an old man sitting at the edge of the forest when I can be out hunting and killing."

"You've used my hunting tactics to kill for sport," replied Grandpa. "Not what I taught you, that's for sure." Grandpa turned to the other men. "Can you assure me this man will not be able to threaten my granddaughter again? If not, I will need to call the police and have him arrested."

"We will make sure he doesn't come back," said Bob. "Don't worry about that. We are leaving now and will make sure he stays with us at our camp until sunrise, when we will leave the conservation area. I think this is just a big misunderstanding, and we will make sure he does not return."

"Thank you," Jenna replied, looking at Bob. "I want to make sure my Ralphie will be safe."

"You little lying . . ." started Ike, but he was cut off by Mitch.

"Okay, Ike," Mitch stated. "We have had enough of your lies. First a dragon, now a girl that turns into a wolf. She doesn't look frightening to me. You will come with us now—and stay with us until we leave tomorrow—or we will let this man call the police. What is your answer? Yes or no. We will not be discussing your ridiculous imaginary creatures any longer."

"Okay, I will leave with you and stay at camp," sulked Ike. "You don't need to call the police after me." Ike looked back at Jenna and glared, knowing he could not say anything else, as no one would believe him.

"Thank you," Grandpa directed to Bob. "We'll be going in for the night now and would appreciate if you can please make sure this man stays with you and has no chance to hurt my granddaughter or her pet." He then turned to look at Ike and continued, "Ike, I take threatening my family very seriously, and if I see you again near this house, you can rest assured I will report this incident to the police, and they will want to ask you some very serious questions about pulling a knife on a little girl. Do you understand?"

"Oh, come on," Ike retorted. "You didn't think I would hurt a little girl, do you? I only wanted to scare her a little, teach her a lesson about entering the woods all by herself. It's dangerous."

"That's not what you were acting like earlier," said Mitch, rebuking Ike's casual threat toward Jenna. "Demanding we follow you so you could find this little girl and get her little fox as your prize and claiming she turned into a wolf and bit you. You also forgot to mention pulling a knife on her; a very important detail in your story. Let's go everyone," Mitch said as he turned toward the woods. The four others followed behind, making sure Ike was with them. About half-way back to the woods, he turned back to Grandpa. Mitch continued, "and don't worry about Ike. He will not be back; I guarantee it."

Mitch turned and glared at Ike. "You will not be causing any more problems here, or anywhere else if I have anything to do with it." Ike said nothing, but the look in his eyes as he glared at Jenna reminded her of the look Ranco gave her as the hunters chased him out of their camp; he was going to get even with her, no matter what.

Grandpa and Jenna remained quiet as the men walked back into the woods, arguing with Ike about why he had tricked them to come out on a wild goose hunt.

As the hunters got out of earshot, Grandpa turned to Jenna and whispered, "Let's get inside before they change their minds and come back." Grandpa glanced over to where Ituria had last been seen and could barely see him blended into the forest darkness. He nodded his head at Ituria, not wanting to speak in case the hunters were still close enough to hear, and Ituria nodded back.

Jenna whispered, "Okay," and picked up Ralphie and followed Grandpa onto the porch. The screened-in porch had a table and a few chairs. Jenna sat down in one of the chairs and set Ralphie down on the floor.

"Ralphie," Jenna said as she held his head in her hands. "I am so glad you are safe now. You will have to stay here tonight. You can't go back into the woods tonight. I don't want any chance of you getting caught in another trap!"

"You are right," Ralphie agreed. "I would feel much safer here with you tonight."

"Let me go in and get some blankets, as well as some food and water for you, so you can get comfortable," Jenna said as she stood up to go inside.

"Is everything okay?" Sandy whispered as she peaked out the door. "What was happening before?" she asked a little louder as she stepped onto the porch. She stopped in her tracks as she realized there was a fox on the porch. "Where did that come from?"

"Don't you remember," Jenna replied. "told you he is my pet fox; I have had him for a few years now—remember?" Jenna moved closer to Sandy and whispered, "We have to protect him from the hunters...they want to kill him and skin him for a trophy." As Jenna spoke, Sandy could hear the conviction in her voice; she would do whatever was necessary to protect this small animal.

"Oh no," Sandy exclaimed as she saw his back paw. "He's hurt! What happened?"

"The hunters set up a trap," Jenna explained. "They were going to kill him, skin him, and leave his body to rot in the forest. . ." Jenna paused as she tried to forget the vivid memories of a few minutes ago. "He's my friend, and I would not let that happen. Please don't tell Mom and Dad tonight; tomorrow the hunters will be gone and Ralphie can go home again."

"Here you go, Ralphie," said Grandpa as he walked back onto the porch. A warm blanket, some cheese filled crackers, and a bowl of water filled his hands. Grandpa laid out everything and Ralphie ate some crackers and drank some water.

"You make yourself comfortable here on the porch, Ralphie," Grandpa continued. "I will stay with you tonight. We will see how you feel in the morning, whether we need to take you to a vet or not."

Grandpa turned to Jenna and continued, "You have had a long day, why don't you go ahead inside and get some sleep. By tomorrow morning the hunters will be gone, and this will be over."

Jenna nodded; she was exhausted. The stress of the last few hours had drained her strength and she felt weak. "Okay," she agreed. "If you will be okay out here, you'll need a blanket, and you have to promise to wake me if you need anything, anything at all."

Grandpa nodded. "Don't you worry about Ralphie and me. We will be fine. Now get inside before your parents wake up and get worried."

He turned to Sandy. "You too, everyone needs to get some sleep. We can talk in the morning."

Chapter Eighteen

SOMETHING IS WRONG

Jenna felt drained and needed some sleep. Grandpa should be okay on the porch with Ralphie, and the hunters had promised they would keep Ike away and leave the area first thing in the morning. As she walked to her bedroom, she wondered, *will I have trouble falling asleep?* But as soon as she laid in her bed, still wearing her day clothes, she fell into a deep, deep slumber.

Ike's voice haunted her dreams, and her dreams turned into a nightmare. She could hear him yelling the fox was his, he would get him no matter what anyone else said.

Suddenly Jenna sat up straight in her bed, wide awake. She did not know what time it was but could tell it was close to dawn. Something was wrong. She didn't know what or why she felt this way, but something was wrong. She had to make sure Ralphie was okay, as her dreams of Ike hurting Ralphie were too vivid, too real.

She quietly walked onto the back porch. The lights were low, so it was difficult to see where Ralphie and Grandpa were.

"Grandpa…Ralphie…where are you?" she whispered. "Is everything okay?"

No answer. "Grandpa, Ralphie, is everything okay?" she whispered again.

"Jenna," she heard a small voice whisper back. It was Sedric, the squirrel who had helped her save Ituria several months ago. Jenna was glad she hadn't changed into her pajamas, so she still had the translator stone in her pocket.

Jenna went out the back porch door, and she could barely see Sedric holding onto the side of the tree. He continued, "Your grandpa and Ralphie have gone into the forest. Your grandpa said he wanted to make sure the hunters had left the area. Ralphie went with him to show him the way. They left a few hours ago. Your grandpa said not to wake you, that you had been through enough. Ituria saw them go and asked me to wait here until you woke up."

"Sedric," Jenna replied. "Do you know what could've happened to them? If they have been gone for hours, something is not right. I feel it."

"I do not know what has happened. Ituria asked me to stay here and tell you not to go out into the forest; it would be too dangerous."

"I have to go. Something is wrong, something has happened to them!" Jenna tried to control the rising panic, trying not to think of the things Ike could do to Grandpa and Ralphie while they were alone in the forest. She knew something was wrong but did not know what. She had to help them. She had to remain calm, though. She could not allow herself to transform into a wolf; that was what Ike was waiting for.

"Jenna," warned Sedric. "Ituria has asked me to make sure you do not go into the forest. Please stay until daylight!"

"No, I can't," she replied. "That will be too late!" Her senses were telling her that action was needed now. Jenna returned to the porch and grabbed the flashlight, then headed out again. "Sedric," she said, "would you go with me? You can ride on my shoulder and jump into the trees if any-thing should happen. I could use another set of eyes and ears out there. I can't turn into a wolf; that would be the worst thing, and just what Ike would want."

"If you must go, of course I will help," he replied, jumping onto Jenna's shoulder. "I will do what I can, but Ituria said it would be best if you did not go into the forest now."

"Ituria does not understand humans like Ike the way I do," Jenna replied. "Ike will not stop until he has done everything he can to prove that he was right—even if it means killing my grandpa and Ralphie in the process. I know he is probably setting a trap for me, but I can't sit around here and wait another second. I hope you can understand." The urgent tone of Jenna's voice told Sedric that trying to convince her to stay was useless.

"I will help in any way I can," Sedric answered, "and maybe we can get more help as we go toward the hunters' camp. Ituria did give me this to give to you. I'm not sure what it is, but he said to use it only in the direst of circumstances, as its effect cannot be reversed."

"Thanks, Sedric," Jenna replied. "I appreciate your help and companionship. Together, I know we can save Grandpa and Ralphie!" Jenna picked up the small object Sedric had in his paw. It looked like a large acorn or seed. She was not sure what it was for, but if Ituria wanted her to have it, she would keep it. She may find herself in circumstances that would require she use it, although she was not sure how.

Jenna, with Sedric on her shoulder, headed off into the forest. Jenna used the flashlight to follow her grandpa's tracks.

"Sedric," she said. "Please listen carefully for any human sounds moving through the bushes, or other noises. Let me know if you hear anything out of the ordinary."

They moved as quietly as possible, walking for about twenty minutes, following Grandpa's footprints in the path through the forest. Suddenly, Jenna got the feeling she should stop. She couldn't describe why, but she stopped and moved behind a tree. "Jenna," whispered Sedric. "What is wrong?"

Jenna put her finger to her mouth, signaling Sedric to be quiet. They waited in silence. In the far distance she could hear something. She was not sure what it was, but it was not a normal sound to hear in the forest a night. It sounded like someone or something was purposefully trying to draw attention to itself. Could it be Grandpa, needing help? Or could it be Ike, trying to draw her into a trap? Or both? Jenna could not tell, but she and Sedric would not walk on the path anymore and would stay hidden in the trees as they tried to approach the sound that was made to draw her in.

Jenna walked behind the trees lining the path. Her feet searching for soft sand or grass, making sure not to step on any branches that would make noise as she walked. After a few minutes, Sedric tapped her on the shoulder, pointed to himself, then the tree. Jenna stopped and nodded her head. Sedric leaped into the tree, trying to see if he could see anything up the path. He shook his head and jumped back onto her shoulder, and they continued.

The noises grew louder, and she could now hear faint human voices. She could not understand the words, only a conversation going on, people arguing about something. Slowly and carefully, they moved closer, making sure not to make any noises themselves.

Once again, Sedric tapped her shoulder, then jumped onto the tree. This time he could see something and ran up the tree a little further to get a better look. After a minute, he ran down and scurried back onto Jenna's shoulder.

"Jenna," he whispered. "It's Ike and your grandpa. They are arguing. It looks like Ralphie is there also, chained to a tree. There is a fire going and Ike is standing, looking out into the forest. He must be waiting for you to show up."

Jenna crouched to the ground. It was as she feared; Ike was holding Grandpa and Ralphie, waiting for her to show up. *What can I do? What would work?* She thought getting closer might give her a clue, if she could hear what they were talking about, so she went a little closer; just enough to be able to understand the conversation.

"...but we can wait here, no problem, she will show up sooner or later," said Ike.

"No, your hunter friends will know you are missing and come looking for you. They will find you first." *It's Grandpa.*

"No way, they will be sleeping for a while," replied Ike with a laugh.

"But how did you escape from the other hunters? They promised me you would not go back into the woods."

"It was easy," Ike said. "I just slipped something in their coffee, and they all went to sleep like babies! You can't cage Ike Monnihan! I am the best! So now all we do is wait for your little granddaughter. He laughed menacingly. "I'm sure she will show up to save you and her little fox!"

Jenna though of the options available to her—there would be no help from the hunters, they had been drugged. Ike was waiting for her to show up, no way to sneak up on him. He would hurt Grandpa and Ralphie if she did anything anyway. What could she do?

Chapter Nineteen

IKE'S PRISONERS

Not many choices at this point, Jenna thought. Ike was a trained hunter and had baited her to trap her. She couldn't just walk into the camp like she did last time. There were no other humans to keep Ike from taking his revenge on her for making him look like a fool. She knew he would tie her up or something worse, so she could not get away.

Was there any way to communicate with Grandpa without Ike being aware? What if they go on the opposite side of where Grandpa sat? The fire light would shine in their eyes, and he would know they were there. Ike wouldn't see if he were looking in another direction or at a different angle. The light would only shine in their eyes if they were looking directly at Grandpa across the fire. He would see and understand.

What would they gain from getting Grandpa's attention? He might be able to distract Ike while they free Ralphie. But then, Ike would know something was going on, and Grandpa would still be trapped—can't take that step now. What else could Jenna do? If Grandpa knew she was there, what would he do?

Would he help or would he make things worse, mad at her for coming after him?

Jenna backed away, so she could whisper to Sedric. "Sedric," she started. "Is there anyone around here you could get to help us? I'm thinking we need to trap Ike somehow so we can free Ralphie and Grandpa. Remember the trapper plant Knocker talked about? It sounds like now is the time to use it. We can trap Ike in it, and while he is trying to figure out a way to escape, we can free them. Do you think you could find some friends and bring back one without getting trapped in it yourself?"

Sedric nodded.

Jenna continued, "I'm going to circle around Ike's camp so I will be directly across from Grandpa, so he will see I'm here. At least he will know we are here to help. Please get a trapper plant big enough for us to trap Ike in, and bring it back. And please be careful!"

Sedric took off into the dark, and Jenna slowly and carefully circled around until she was opposite from Grandpa with the fire between them. She then looked at him, waiting for him to glance her way.

She was close enough again to hear Grandpa and Ike were still arguing, with Ike trying to convince Grandpa Jenna was really a wolf.

"I tell you, she turned into a wolf and bit my hand!" Ike argued. "Look at my hand, that wasn't done by some small little fox." Ike unwrapped his hand and showed the teeth marks, which showed a much larger bite than Ralphie could have made.

"But doesn't that sound ridiculous? How would she bite you?" Grandpa replied. "And why would she bite you—what did you do to her?"

"Well, I threatened her little pet over there, probably not the best idea. But I had trapped that fox, fair and square, so it was mine. She shouldn't be out at night. It was dangerous, and I was letting her know she shouldn't be running around at night in the woods. She overreacted, I think, and turned into a giant wolf and bit me."

"I wouldn't have really hurt her with the knife; I was just trying to scare her. You believe me, don't you?" Ike looked at Grandpa and away from where Jenna was hiding. Jenna moved so Grandpa could see her eyes in the dark. Her eyes reflected the fire, telling him she was there. His eyes widened a little, then he quickly looked away, his actions telling Jenna he had gotten the message.

Ike continued to press his argument, trying to get Grandpa on his side. "She should not have been out at night. I was trying to scare her and make her realize she should not be out at night."

"So," said Grandpa, trying to engage Ike in conversation, knowing Jenna would hear, "what do you plan on doing with my granddaughter when you finally catch her? She's only a little girl."

"I'll tell you," Ike snarled. "I'm going to make her show you she's a wolf! I'll scare her again; then she will turn into a wolf again and you'll see I was right. Then everyone will believe me." Ike sounded stressed, ready to crack under the pressure, wanting someone to believe his story.

Grandpa laughed. "I've known my grand-daughter since she was born," he replied. "I have never seen any indication she is a wolf. I think the forest is playing with your mind and you were seeing things that weren't there. What were you doing in the conservation area anyway? Hunting foxes, or even wolves, isn't exactly your main target. Usually you go for bigger things—bear, moose, elephants. Why were you here in this area? What did you need Jenna's little fox for anyway?"

Ike looked at Grandpa for a moment, thinking. Jenna could tell he was trying to decide if he should reveal his real reason for being there. Then he walked over to where Grandpa was sitting and sat down next to him. "I'll tell you," he started, almost whispering, "but it will sound even stranger than Jenna being a wolf. When I was here a few months ago, I saw what looked like a dragon. It came at me after I had shot two wolves who were getting ready to fight. I went to claim the bodies when this large dragon came out and roared at me, and my party ran away at the sound. I returned to catch it. No one would believe me when I told them about it. The rest of my party did not see it. You do believe me, don't you?" Ike was pleading now. "You know the area. You grew up here; maybe you have seen it too. Have you?" Ike was close to Grandpa, staring at him with wild eyes.

Grandpa stared back at Ike, trying to formulate a response. He knew Ike was beyond rationalizing the situation, so he spoke in a soft tone to try and calm him down. "Ike, listen to me. I grew up in these woods. I have seen some large deer on occasion. I have never seen anything bigger than the gators in here, but they are usually in the water and would not be far from the lake. I really do not know what you could be talking about."

"I know what I saw! It wasn't a gator!" Ike stood up and started looking out into the forest. Dawn was breaking, so shadows could be seen moving between the trees as the forest inhabitants were waking up. "I know I saw your granddaughter turn into a wolf too. Ain't no one going to convince me otherwise. You just wait and see. She will come here to rescue you, and I will make her turn into a wolf, then shoot her too!"

"What!" exclaimed Grandpa. "You are going to shoot her? How dare you! What have you become? Listen to yourself. You are delusional. You need to leave this forest now and never come back. Something has happened to you that you are not thinking rationally. I should have called the police last night when I had the chance."

"Yep, you probably should have, but you didn't." Ike smirked. "You don't know who you are dealing with. I won't rest until I prove I was right. If it costs the lives of you and your granddaughter, so what. You shouldn't be wandering in the woods late at night either—lots of things can happen to an old man . . ." Ike stopped talking but glared at Grandpa with an evil grin on his face. "She will maybe come quicker if she hears you or the fox in pain. What do you think? Which should I hurt first?" Ike laughed loudly. "Does it really matter? None of you will survive the day!"

Jenna knew she had to act soon and looked around as she saw Sedric come up beside her. Sedric nodded, confirming he had been able to get a trapper plant. Jenna would need to figure out how to get Ike trapped in it, allowing her to rescue Grandpa and Ralphie. Should she go into the camp, knowing Ike was planning to shoot her? She would need to control her emotions because as soon as she turned into a wolf, she would be shot.

What other option did she have?

Chapter Twenty

PLANNING A TRAP

J enna was running out of time. Ike's words that he was planning on killing them all put her mind in motion. *Something must be done now*, she thought to herself. *I can't wait for the drugged hunters to finally awaken or the forest creatures to help at daylight.*

She backed away a bit from the camp so she could talk with Sedric. "Sedric," she whispered. "Who were you able to find to help you with the trapper plant?"

"There were not many friends out tonight," he replied, "but I was able to find a few out and able to help, as they usually sleep during the day. I don't think you have met them before. Ryan is what you humans call a skunk, and Dexter is what you would refer to as a raccoon. They were both out, and after I explained the situation and your need to rescue Ralphie, they were glad to help."

"Also," Sedric whispered, "Ituria is out there, and he needs you to know…the seed he gave you is *magic*. He is not allowed to interfere in this situation with the human, but said if you need to stop Ike, the magic seed will not kill him, but will make him a part of the forest."

"What does that mean, part of the forest?"

"He did not tell me, but said once it was put into Ike's mouth, the effect could not be reversed, so it should only be used if there were no other alternatives."

"Thank you, Sedric," Jenna whispered back. "Please tell Ituria it will be necessary to use this seed, as Ike is going to kill Ralphie, Grandpa, and me if he gets the chance. He cannot be allowed to leave the forest."

Once Jenna realized she would have to take down Ike to protect her family and friends, she was glad Ituria gave her an option that did not involve killing him. She did not know if she could kill Ike, even if she was able to do so physically in her wolf form. She did not want to become like him, taking another life, even though he had no remorse at the thought of killing them.

Her mind raced back to the present situation. What plan could she come up with to rescue Grandpa and Ralphie before Ike could hurt them. She had the trapper plant, she had a few forest friends, and she had a magic seed which if put in Ike's mouth would keep him from leaving the forest. *This just might work.*

"Sedric," she whispered. "Please get your two friends, Ryan and Dexter. I think we can do this!" Plans formulated in her mind on how everyone could help.

Sedric scurried into the darkness, only to return in less than a minute with Ryan and Dexter.

"Listen carefully. We don't have much time," Jenna whispered as they formed a small circle. "Ryan and Dexter, I am glad to meet you and thank you for agreeing to help free Ralphie and my grandpa."

They nodded in reply, ready to follow her instructions.

"We need to get the trapper plant where I can push Ike into it," she continued. "But we need to keep you far enough away so Ike doesn't see you and try to shoot you. Both of you would normally go out at night, so wouldn't seem suspicious if Ike saw you walk by the outside of his camp. If you could pull the trapper plant over to the north opening in the bushes, and sort of push it into the opening; that would be most helpful."

"Ryan, if Ike should spot you and come toward you for any reason, even just to see what you are doing," Jenna whispered, looking at him, "you need to shoot him with your spray and then disappear as quickly as you can because he will try and hurt you."

"Dexter, once the trapper plant is in place, I need you to go over behind Ralphie and free him from the rope Ike tied him up with. Then you and Ralphie disappear into the forest."

Dexter and Ryan nodded.

"Sedrick you will need to go behind my grandpa and wait to lead him away from camp. I can't give Ike any targets when he realizes what is happening. Don't let Grandpa try and stay to help. Ike wants to kill him to get back at me, and I can't have that happen."

"We are losing the cover of darkness so we must hurry. Anyone have any questions?"

No one spoke, all ready to get on to the tasks at hand.

"Okay, let's go!" she whispered. Jenna tried to sound confident, but while her plan got Ralphie and Grandpa away from Ike, she still wasn't sure how she was going to trap Ike and get the magic seed into his mouth. All she could do was to get everyone else away, then hope for the best.

Chapter Twenty-One

STEP ONE:
SAVING RALPHIE

J enna approached the camp again, across from Grandpa, so if he looked her way, he could see she was back.

Ike was still trying to convince Grandpa of the 'dragon' he saw.

"I'm going to catch that dragon," he continued. "No matter how long it takes or how many times I have to come back to this forest. But first, I'm going to get me a wolf."

Ike looked around. "I'm surprised that little girl ain't here yet. Maybe I need to hurt her little foxie again," he said menacingly. "That little thing squeaks and cries when it is hurt. That will get her here."

Jenna nodded to Ryan and Dexter, and they slowly pulled the trapper plant into the opening at the north of camp. It made a swooshing sound, like something being dragged over grass, and it drew Ike's attention. He stopped talking to Grandpa and walked toward the north side of the campsite.

"Wonder what it could be," he said. "Don't sound like your little girl, but maybe a snake or something."

Ike peered into the darkness. It was not light enough to make out many outlines, so the addition of a flat plant laying outside camp wasn't readily visible.

Jenna remembered Knocker told her the trapper plant was one of the most dangerous plants in Middle Forest. It is shaped like a wide shallow bowl and looks like it is full of fresh water. But if an animal tries to drink the water, it gets trapped by the gooey liquid in the plant and is slowly digested by the plant.

The glue was so strong that nothing, not even the large animals, could pull away. If she could get Ike's hands trapped in it, he would not be able to use a gun or knife to hurt them. That would be the best way to trap him. However, it was no longer connected to the ground, so she would need to tie Ike up or keep him from moving once he fell on it.

"Where is that little foxie friend of hers?" Ike said. "I know what to do to get her close. That's how to get the larger prey in, hurt their little ones! That's something you didn't teach me—I learned it myself!" Ike was laughing hysterically now, and Jenna knew she couldn't remain hidden any longer. Dexter was with Ralphie now and Ike could not see them. She needed to buy them another minute or two.

"Grandpa!" she shouted as she stepped into the camp. "What are you doing out so early! I've been looking all over for you. You know I get worried when you wander about. Mom and Dad said you can't take walks through the woods anymore without someone to go with you."

"Jenna," Grandpa exclaimed. "What are you doing away from home? You were supposed to stay there and be safe from all the hunters running around. You need to get out of here. It's a trap!"

But Ike was having no part of it. "Both of you, sit yourselves down now!" Ike shouted. "And don't you two get near each other. We got some talking to do, and no whispering to each other about what is going on. You, little lady, or should I say little wolf, go sit down away from him."

Jenna went over to the north side of the clearing where Dexter and Ryan had left the trapper plant, so to draw Ike's attention away from Ralphie, who was on the opposite side. Dexter should be with Ralphie now and could hopefully get him loose and away from camp.

"Now, let's have a cozy little talk about why you are out here, shall we?" said Ike in a nasty tone.

"I saw my grandpa was not in the house, and I came out to find him," Jenna replied. "He's not as young as he once was and might need help or have gotten lost in the forest."

"You mean you weren't looking for your little foxie?"

Jenna glanced quickly over to where she knew Ralphie had been tied up. She saw two sets of eyes reflecting from the fire, and they appeared to nod and then disappear. *Ralphie is safe!*

Jenna looked at Grandpa. "Grandpa, did you bring Ralphie out with you? I thought I saw him sleeping in his bed. His foot was swollen. We will have to get him to the vet in the morning."

Grandpa looked at Jenna and nodded. "Yes, I left Ralphie in his bed. I'm not sure what Ike is talking about."

Jenna was relieved Grandpa had understood she had gotten Ralphie away from the area.

"What are you to talking about!" Ike screamed. "I got that little varmint right here!" Ike stomped over to the south side of the camp and pulled back a bush where he had tied up Ralphie. There was nothing there except a rope!

"What have you done!" he screamed, this time directly at Jenna. "I know I had your little foxie, and so do you and your grandpa." Ike turned and glared at Grandpa. "You know I had her fox You were carrying it when I found you, weren't you? Don't you lie to me!"

Chapter Twenty-Two

Step Two:
Saving Grandpa

Grandpa remained calm and said, "I don't know what you are talking about. I was taking a walk in the forest when you surprised me and brought me to this camp. I would not have brought a wounded animal into the forest."

Ike was livid, his face turning bright red as he started toward Grandpa, shouting, "You know you had that fox. Why we was just talking about how I planned to hurt him to force your little grand-daughter to show up!"

"You were going to do what?" Jenna shouted, drawing attention back to herself.

Ike turned away from Grandpa, then stomped toward Jenna, stopping a few feet away as an evil grin appeared on his face. "I don't need your little foxy anymore. He was just bait! Why don't you shift back into a wolf, and I'll deal with you?"

She knew she needed to get Ike to the north side of the camp and keep him from hurting Grandpa. Since she had taken all of his ammunition, the only weapon he would have now would be the knife, but it was a large knife and he could kill them both easily if they were not careful. Keeping with the plan, Sedric would be waiting to take Grandpa away when he saw the chance.

"What makes you think you can come into this forest and just hurt anything you want?" She wanted to engage Ike into dialogue. "This forest does not want you here. It has been peaceful for a long time. You need to leave and never come back." Jenna tried to sound strong, hoping Ike could not hear any weakness in her voice.

"Well, little girl, you think you can take me on? Granted, your grandpa is an old man, and he would not be a problem to kill, and I could make it so no one would ever find his body. That okay with you? Or do you want to be the first one to go? I need you to turn into a wolf again, so we can fight."

Ike pulled out his knife, the long hunting knife he had used earlier to threaten Jenna and Ralphie. The fire reflected in the blade, making it look more sinister as he waved it around in the air.

Jenna glanced quickly to the east side of camp where Grandpa had been, and he was no longer there. She looked back at Ike as he was slowly approaching, smiling with glee at the prospect of killing her once she got mad enough to change into a wolf.

"Okay," Jenna said calmly, knowing Grandpa was safe too. "You will not get away with killing anyone, you know that, right?"

"Oh, but I will. I will make you turn into a wolf and then kill you in front of your grandpa, and then him next. I will have my trophy, and you will be dead!" Ike laughed and continued toward her.

Jenna backed up, getting closer to the trapper plant. She knew she could not get caught in it, but needed to get the knife hand trapped, then push the rest of him in. She tried to resist changing into a wolf, but the threats against Grandpa were welling up inside and she really wanted Ike to be gone. She knew he would never stop trying to hurt Grandpa, and she could not allow that.

Jenna looked behind her quickly and saw the trapper plant was only a few feet away. If she allowed herself to turn into a wolf, Ike would lunge at her, and if she jumped out of the way, he would land in the trap. That was the only thing she could concentrate on to keep her human.

Now she was close enough to let her anger out. "You will not kill anyone or anything else, ever!" Jenna wanted to make sure Ike was so focused on her he didn't notice Grandpa was gone. She knew Ike would react quickly as she turned into a wolf, so she had to be ready.

"Hey, look, your little granddaughter has some spirit. It will be fun to kill her!" said Ike as he turned to look at Grandpa. He stopped when he realized Grandpa was gone.

"Where did he go?" Ike screamed at Jenna.

"He's not there, never was. You have made up the whole story in your head. Dragons, girls who turn into wolves, everything." Jenna could see Ike was over the edge at this point. "No going back now. You were willing to kill my grandpa to get your trophy. What does it make you? A murderer! How can you live with yourself—all the animals you killed for sport or to hang on a wall. They were living creatures; they had lives and families, just like humans do!"

"You are still here," Ike sniped. "You are real, and I will kill you. Why not turn into your little wolf self to make it a fair fight?"

"So be it!" Jenna said, and she released all the emotions she had been suppressing for the last few minutes. She could feel the forest changing her into a wolf, and as she changed, she shouted, "Come and get me!"

Chapter Twenty-Three

FINAL CONFRONTATION

Jenna, in her wolf form, quickly bounded out of the north side of the camp, careful not to step into the trapper plant. As soon as she passed over it and got out of Ike's line of sight, she stopped and turned, waiting for Ike to follow.

Ike was too mad now to do anything other than follow her. As he came after her, she jumped on him, knocking him to the ground, both his arms landing in the trapper plant. They were instantly immobilized, and he was laying on the ground, struggling to get himself free. As he struggled, he splashed the gluey substance around, getting it on his face and legs also. Branches, leaves, dirt, all started to cover him as he rolled on the ground.

Jenna stayed clear, watching as he struggled. She knew she would have to become a human again to put the seed in his mouth, but she needed to make sure he was unable to move before she did so.

"Jenna . . ." A voice came up behind her; it was Grandpa, still holding his translation stone. "What will you do now? He has seen you turn into a wolf."

"Grandpa," she growled. "We cannot let him leave the forest. You heard him; he will not stop until he has killed you and me and found his dragon."

"But what will you do? Will you become like him and kill him?"

"No" Jenna replied. "I cannot kill him. I did not think I could unless I had to, to protect you."

"You wimpy little kid," Ike screamed. "When I get myself out of this, I will kill you both, and there's nothing you can do about it—you don't have the strength to kill something—takes strength to take a life." Ike started struggling again and was almost covered with the gluey liquid. Sticks and dirt covered him.

"What will you do?" Grandpa repeated. "Leave him like this and let something else kill him?"

"If something else killed him they would get trapped in the glue and would die also. If we left him and his hunting party found him, they might figure out a way to free him, and that is not acceptable either. Ituria told me a way to make him stay in the forest forever without killing him. I hope it will work. However, I need to turn back into a human to accomplish it. Before I do, we need to make sure he can't move or get at his knife."

"Grandpa," Jenna continued. "I'm going to pull some branches over, and I need you to push them on top of Ike, to hold him down. You can't get close enough for Ike to splash you with the glue. Then I can change back to human form. Can you do that?"

"Yes," he replied. "I can. Let's make it happen."

"Wimpy girl can't kill me, then you will never be rid of me. I will be back every chance I get. You can count on that!" Ike sounded scared but was defiant, realizing Jenna did have a weakness. She wasn't a heartless killer like he was. "I will have no problem killing you, so watch your back!"

Jenna and Grandpa said nothing further and worked together to put several large branches on Ike's legs to keep him from moving. Ike was yelling and screaming the whole time, but they ignored his ranting. Now he could not move his arms or legs. His face was sideways on the ground, but he could still talk. Knowing Jenna was not going to kill him made him arrogant.

"Don't you worry. I will get you. I know where you live. You will never be rid of me!" Ike continued.

"Jenna," Grandpa said. "He cannot move. You need to hurry, as it will be daylight soon and the drugs will be wearing off the other hunters."

"You are right." Jenna sat on the ground and tried to focus.

Ike was yelling in the background, but she would not listen. She had to turn back into a human to complete her task. She could feel Ituria was close, but knew he was unable to assist. It was up to her. She closed her eyes and thought of Grandpa, Ralphie, her family, her animal friends, and she needed to remain calm to protect them all.

Moments later, she was human again and felt for the large seed in her pocket.

"See, I told you, you are a coward," Ike chided. "What are you going to do now, run . . ."

Jenn quickly took the seed and shoved it into Ike's mouth while he was talking and backed away before he could splash the glue on her.

Ike looked at Jenna, first with anger, then surprise. He was not sure what was happening and tried to spit it out, but he couldn't.

Jenna and Grandpa backed away a little further, to see what was going to happen, what the seed would do to him.

Ike was changing, transforming into something, but they were not sure what. The fire was too far away to give much light, and dawn was not light enough either to fully show the transformation. The tree branches Jenna and Grandpa had placed on Ike's legs rolled away. Ike was now in a standing position, still covered with sticks, leaves, and dirt; his hands still stuck in the trapper plant.

Slowly, his figure took the shape of a tree, stretching skyward, his branches forming as he grew taller and taller. His hunter's knife fell to the ground at the base of the tree with a soft thud as it landed in the leaves. Ike would not need it anymore. Ike had become part of the forest and would not leave again. Jenna thought it was a fitting punishment; he could watch the animals roam the forest but would not be able to hurt them anymore.

Jenna turned to Grandpa and gave him a hug, then she asked quietly, "Why did you come out into the forest, knowing Ike might be out here?"

"I was hoping I could talk some sense into him," he replied. "But Ike was too far gone. I am glad you found a way to stop him without killing him."

117

Ituria stepped out of the forest darkness. "I too am glad you were successful in controlling yourself in order to resolve your issues with Ike without resorting to killing him." He must have been watching everything from a distance.

"Jenna, you used the reflection of the fire in your eyes to communicate with your Grandfather; but today I have also seen that you have a fire in your heart, that you have the courage to defend my forest and its creatures. My deepest thanks to you. You will be remembered for your bravery tonight."

Ituria turned to look toward the hunters' camp, then continued, "But now, I need to tell you the other members of the hunting party have awakened, and are now in the forest, looking for Ike. You must be prepared." Ituria faded back into the forest once again.

It was light enough now to see the tree Ike had become. It was a tall, strong tree with many branches. Ike would be able to live a long life, but he would not be able to kill innocent animals anymore. There was no sign of Ike's clothes. They had been absorbed in the making of the tree, so no one would be able to tell it was connected to Ike. Jenna picked up the hunting knife and threw it into the fire. There was no time to try and hide that Ike had been here, and the hunters would be tracking him to this spot.

"Grandpa," she said quietly. "Let's leave now and return home before the hunting group gets here."

Grandpa nodded, and they both turned to the east to go home. Dexter came up to them as they walked. "I can lead you home now, so you don't get lost. Ralphie showed me where you live."

"Dexter," Jenna replied softly. "Thanks so much for your help in freeing Ralphie. I do appreciate it. I'm glad you were able to help him get to somewhere safe."

"I was glad to help. Though Ralphie and I are out and about at different times, we do see each other on occasion, and he is my friend. He told me you were here to help the animals who live in the forest, so I was glad to do my part."

They walked quietly back to Jenna's house, so as not to attract any attention to themselves.

As the first rays of sunlight broke through the forest canopy, Jenna and Grandpa made it back to the house. While it was not a long walk for Jenna, she could tell Grandpa was tired. Jenna turned to Dexter. "Thanks again, my new friend. Take care of yourself. The hunters are still in the forest a little longer."

Dexter nodded and said, "Glad to help!" As Ralphie stood up and walked over to Jenna, Dexter continued, "Hi, Ralphie, hope you are feeling better soon!" He then turned and scampered back into the forest. Jenna and Grandpa headed onto the porch with Ralphie and sat down, a welcome rest after the walk back.

"Are you okay, Grandpa?" Jenna asked.

"I'm a little tired, but I'll be fine," Grandpa replied. "I could use a little rest."

"Okay, we will all take a rest here on the porch, sounds like a good plan." Jenna helped Grandpa get comfortable and got him a chair to prop up his feet so he could take a nap. He was asleep in a few minutes but not Jenna. She couldn't help but think of what had transpired over the last few hours and wonder what would happen next.

Chapter Twenty-Four

SAFE AT LAST

I t was only a few minutes before Jenna's thoughts were interrupted by noises coming out of the forest, branches breaking, footsteps in the leaves, and people talking loudly.

She looked from the porch back into the woods and saw several men walking toward the house. It looked like the men who had been here last night.

"Hi in there," one of them shouted. "Can you come out here for a minute?"

Jenna stayed on the porch and shouted back, "What's the matter?"

"It's me, Bob, from last night. We need to make sure you and your Grandpa are okay."

Jenna went outside of the porch, so Grandpa would not wake up.

"Hi," she said. "We are fine. We stayed up with my fox last night, and we are resting here on the porch. What's the matter?"

"Somehow Ike was able to give us some type of sleeping medicine and got away. We don't know where he went, and thought he might head here, based on his actions last night."

"We've been on the porch all night with Ralphie, and Ike has not been here," Jenna replied.

"Okay, that's good," Bob continued. "We found someone had started a fire a few miles from here and thought he might be planning to come this way. Please be on the lookout for him, and if you do see him, I would suggest calling the police. He does not seem to have his senses about him anymore. He kept rambling on and on about a dragon and a wolf the whole walk back to camp last night."

"Thanks for the warning. We appreciate it. We will look out for him and call the police if he comes this way."

"You know, Bob," joked Mitch. "My guess is he was so embarrassed he took off last night and we'll never see him again."

Jenna smiled and said, "I hope you are right."

"Bye, little girl. Keep safe and stay out of the forest, okay?" said Bob.

"Okay, thanks!" Jenna replied as the men turned and walked away, then turned and headed back toward the porch.

Grandpa watched as she reached the porch door. "Good job, young lady," he said after the hunters were out of earshot. "I don't think we need to worry any more about Ike. You do make a formidable

122

wolf, though. Ituria was right, you have the courage to do what is right. And clever too, using the firelight to let me know you were there."

"You taught me that trick when you told me about the baby gators, remember?" Jenna replied.

"Yes, I do," Grandpa said, smiling. "See, at my age I still have a trick or two to share."

Getting serious again, he continued, "I am glad you decided not to take Ike's life; not to become like him. Killing is a hard thing; once you get used to it, your heart hardens. Especially if you do it for profit or sport. I admit I killed animals in my time, but it was to feed my family, and not to hang something on the wall or make a pile of money."

"Grandpa," Jenna said. "When you have rested up a bit, I would love to hear of your stories with Ituria and Knocker, and the other animals you might have met in Middle Forest."

Grandpa's eyes shined as he looked at Jenna. "I have not told anyone my stories about Knocker and Ituria. No one would believe them anyway, but I would love to tell you. I have lots of stories and adventures to tell."

"I can't wait to hear!" Jenna said excitedly, smiling back.

Suddenly, the back door of the house opened, and Sandy stepped out onto the porch.

"So there you are, you two," called Sandy, pretending to scold but with a smile on her face. "I couldn't find you in the house and was getting worried. I'm so glad you two weren't out roaming the forest this morning. Why not come in and have some breakfast? What does your little fox eat? I'll get him something too."

"Breakfast sounds great!" Jenna replied. "I'll find something for Ralphie."

Jenna and Grandpa smiled at each other as they stood up and followed Sandy inside. Bending over to pick up Ralphie, Jenna thought, *I can't wait to hear about Grandpa's stories of his adventures with Ituria and Knocker!*

THE END

NOTE FROM THE AUTHOR

Although this is a fantasy fiction adventure, hunting for sport is something that humans do every day. I can understand why people hunt for food, as humans have been doing that for thousands of years; however, I have difficulty in understanding why shooting something just to cut off its head to hang on a wall is considered "a sport". In a world where climate change, pollution, and deforestation kill so many animals, adding hunting animals for "sport" seems very unsportsmanlike. Unfortunately, it is a thriving business around the world, driving many species to the brink of extinction.

Wolves in the United States roamed far and wide for thousands of years, until a federally sponsored wolf eradication effort in the early 20th century wiped out most of the population. Biologists have documented that wolves, as the top of the food chain, play a vital role in sustaining viable ecosystems, including preventing deer and elk from over-browsing plants, and their presence improves ecosystems for all inhabitants.

After being declared an endangered species in the 1970s, grey wolves have just started making a comeback, yet their survival is still in question. They were recently removed from the endangered species list in October 2020, and the hunting has once again begun in earnest. In January 2020, wildlife officials identified the first wolf pack seen in Colorado in over a century; unfortunately, most of this first pack were shot and killed as they crossed the state line into Wyoming, where it is legal to kill grey wolves for any reason, or for no reason at all, in 85% of that state.

Many non-profit agencies, such as Defenders of Wildlife, work to protect and defend animals who have no voice of their own. They have recently reported that the State of Colorado has voted to have wolves reintroduced into the state in 17 million acres of public land in the Rocky Mountains. For more information on the great progress made in Colorado for the reintroduction of wolves, see the article "Coloradans Say Yes to Wolves" in the Defenders of Wildlife Magazine – Winter 2021; and get additional information on wolf reintroduction located at: 2020.08 -Restoring Wolves to Colorado–Getting Here–Why reintroduction is the best way to reestablish a self-sustaining wolf population_0.pdf (defenders.org)

Discover more by
JB Moonstar

Chronicles of Ituria

Russ and The Hidden Voice

Taylor and the Red Wolf Rescue

Jenna and the Legend of the White Wolf

Jenna and the Eyes of Fire

Jan and the Secret Cave

Jan and the Search for Lilya

Taylor and the Final Nine

Michelle and the Missing Manatee

Jenna and the Broken Promise

Sara and the Secret Mission

& More Adventures to Come!

The Mermaids of Crystal Cay

Kimmi and the Sea Dragon

Roselia and the Ancient Warriors

& More Adventures to Come!

Coloring Book from
Artist Jenn Kotick

Mermaids

ABOUT THE
AUTHOR

J.B. moved to Florida in her early teens and has lived there ever since, enjoying the mild weather and abundance of wildlife. She even spent several seasons raising orphan squirrels. She graduated from the University of Central Florida and has spent her working career in the legal profession. Her novels are inspired by her family and nature, as well as her need to escape from the real world once in a while.

www.facebook.com/J.B.Moonstar

Instagram
@J.B.Moonstar

Twitter
@jb_moonstar

jbmoonstar.author@gmail.com

www.jbmoonstar.com

Book Club Questions

1. Why did Ituria send Ralphie to find Jenna?

2. Why did Jenna's parents and grandfather leave for the day?

3. Are there plants (or animals) that catch their prey by using glue or other sticky-stuff?

4. Why are there very few plants living in caves? What is missing that most plants need?

5. What does nocturnal mean?

6. Why does Jenna need help from nocturnal animals?

7. Why do some animals sleep during the day and search for food a night?

8. How do trees protect themselves from being eaten by animals?

9. How does Ike get away from the other hunters to set a trap for Jenna?

10. If all wolves are removed from an area, what happens to the other residents?

11. Something to think about—If the wild ecosystem has no top predator and there are too many plant eaters who consume all available vegetation, including smaller trees, what happens to the balance in the ecosystem—where will beavers get trees to build their dams? Where will birds build their nests?

**Discover more at
4HorsemenPublications.com**

10% off using HORSEMEN10

www.ingramcontent.com/pod-product-compliance
Lightning Source LLC
Chambersburg PA
CBHW050413110726
47899CB00008B/2692